I0589957

# MISS ELSPETH'S DESIRE

THE SEARCH DUOLOGY BOOK 1

IMOGENE NIX

Copyright © 2018 by Imogene Nix

All rights reserved.

This book is a work of fiction. All character, places and events are from the author's imagination and should not be confused with fact. Any resemblance to persons, living or dead, events or places is purely coincidental.

No part of this book may be reproduced in any form or by any electronic or mechanical means, including information storage and retrieval systems, without written permission from the author, except for the use of brief quotations in a book review.

Print ISBN: 9780648120551

# DEDICATION

*M*iss Elspeth's Desire has sat, bubbling away in my psyche for so long! I'm not sure exactly when the initial concept for the book began, but the initial states of the manuscript date from 2014 before my sojourn from writing. It was such a joy to complete this labour of love, especially as it's my first historical and required so much historical research.

Elspeth and Aeddan also gave me the opportunity to dabble in some really interesting aspects of sexuality (particularly Tantra) and to investigate the use of the Kama Sutra through the ages and particularly it's place in the boudoir. Elspeth, while a fairly forward and modern woman for her time, evolved in a period when suffragettes were already making themselves heard, and Victorian society was wrestling with great changes. The Indian uprisings surged forward leading to their disaffection in the 1840's leading to their rebellion against the restraints of colonialism, with independence achieved in 1947.

I hope you'll allow me the leeway as I've tinkered (just a tiny bit) with dates and times, though all the main player—including Lord Lytton and the Emir— were indeed in place during the time I've written about.

I look forward to hearing your thoughts on Aeddon and Elspeth's tale and plan to have Isabelle's available soon!

Until next time,

Imogene

# CHAPTER 1

The house was silent, save the ticking of the clock in the hall.

Elspeth Forster sat in the drawing room of the house she shared with her two younger sisters, Isabelle and Louisa. The morning sun peeked through the mullioned windows, and she soaked up the rays, letting them warm her cold body.

*Winter seems to have lasted forever.*

With care, she rose and placed the book she'd been inspecting on the small table beside her chair. Elspeth brushed down the bodice of her green gown and straightened the tiny, cream, silk bows. Her gown fit perfectly. In her mind she conjured up the vision she'd seen this morning in her looking glass of a tall, large-breasted woman. Absently, she glanced beyond the glass panes to the place she'd rather be...the water.

Elspeth schooled her face, ensuring it betrayed none of her frustration as she padded over the floors. She wanted to be outside or at the very least down at her office near the wharf. At the passing of their father, three years previously, she and her sisters had inherited Forster Shipping, and that had become the saving grace of her cloying life.

*If only I'd been born a boy!* She sighed. Sadly, she hadn't, and she had to accept the restrictions of her gender.

She and Isabelle had been debating calling their manager home to discuss business. Of course, she'd also discarded that thought—their inability to meet with the man here stemmed from their younger sister, Louisa's, soon-to-be happy situation because the gently born didn't participate in *trade*. If he were here when Louisa's prospective suitor was, well that would just be a step too far, likely for the union.

The restriction that required both herself and Isabelle to remain *at home* chafed Elspeth in particular. A new shipment of silks were due. Spices too, she'd noted in the ledger yesterday. Her enquiring mind demanded she be among the first to gaze on the prize, to inhale the subtle echoes of scents from remote locations which remained on the cloth—something both she and her sister gained a vicarious pleasure from—before the rich bounty was shipped off to locales throughout the length of England.

Isabelle, who was the only person that knew how restricted she felt, touched her hand. "'Tis only because of our advanced ages, Elspeth. We must be thankful that our father was enlightened enough to allow us to inherit the shipping business. That gives us the opportunity to enjoy such things as come via our ships."

Elspeth stilled at the window, considering Isabelle's strained words. Her mind tossed them over as she inspected the glittering ocean, soothing herself.

"I'd rather be inspecting the incoming cargo." Hunger filled her words. The silks fascinated her. Touching them, knowing that no one else in this country had seen them before her. It fed the emptiness that seemed to grow year upon year.

No one else would understand, or allow her to express her vain wishes...except Isabelle.

"You've been cooped up inside for too long, Elspeth. As have I."

She inclined her head. Isabelle's words rang true, in that they were stuck here in the house until the matter of Louisa's future was settled. Their sister Louisa eagerly awaited a call from her suitor, Mr. Jeremy Lavenwood, at any time, and they were hopeful that he would make an offer for her hand.

*Please let that be today!*

He was the third son of a local squire and quite over his head for their sister. Just as she was for him. Jeremy was an acceptable match for a captain's daughter. Not so high that she would be uncomfortable in the society he kept, but not so low that he would be embarrassed by her trade-immured connections.

He had the added bonus of Louisa's dowry. Their father had settled three thousand pounds on each of his daughters. A significant amount by anyone's standards.

Vibration filled the air beside her. Elspeth half-turned to see a look she'd never before noted on her sister's countenance.

"I was thinking, Elspeth, perhaps if this all comes to pass... Maybe you and I could make a tour of our trading routes? It would help us to strengthen our plans for the future. We'd be able to learn more, and possibly choose things that men of trade might pass over." Isabelle's voice was careful, as if she fought off excitement at the idea. She lowered herself into a nearby seat as she stared at Elspeth.

Elspeth stilled. She weighed her sister's words. *Could they?* Her stomach trembled with anticipation at the thought.

*Adventure. We could travel.*

She looked swiftly toward Isabelle, who waited, her entire body tense, where she'd perched herself on the edge of the chaise. She understood the banked fire in her sister. Elspeth felt the sense of excitement too.

"Perhaps we could discuss this...but later, I think."

Isabelle's gaze shuttered, and Elspeth reached out, briefly touching her sister's hand before drawing back.

"It does have merit, Isabelle. Yet we must look to Louisa first."

She spoke carefully as the heavy wood door swung open and their sister entered the room.

Louisa's demure gown of gold and cream brocade suited her coloring and the tumble of thick, brown hair elegantly piled atop her head. She smiled and fluttered into the seat by Isabelle, adjusting her shawl. This lifestyle suited their youngest sister admirably.

"Mr. Lavenwood should be here soon." Louisa's tone betrayed her excitement.

Elspeth felt a pang of envy, which she squashed quickly. Her sister would stay here within the confines of this small community. Louisa was happy to settle down with a nice, young man. She'd be happy, content even, to marry, raise children, and remain in this tiny settlement. For Elspeth and Isabelle though, it was cloying.

Elspeth had noted the connection between the couple, including the long glances and charming blushes, many months ago. She'd fanned the interest in her sister, encouraged the match, and hopefully it was about to come to pass. Pleasure, vicarious though it was, filled Elspeth at her sister's good fortune.

In her younger years, she'd yearned for someone to offer for her. She'd dreamed of setting up her own house, but as the years had rolled on that dream had withered and died. Now there'd be no wedding in the local chapel for her. She was past her prime, and no man could possibly want her.

At seven and twenty, she knew that to be the truth. Her sister, Isabelle, had shared her fate. *Spinster aunt.* That was the best she —they—could hope for.

The idea of traveling offered a new source of pleasure. It would soothe the craving of her soul. Elspeth turned away, so her back warmed from the heat of the sun.

The view of a ship, sails furled, at the dock had suddenly become too much. The ship was likely one of the Forster fleet. If she'd been born a male, it would have been her right to captain it.

To travel to far-flung places and interact with the world. She wanted to travel, feel the sway of the decks beneath her feet. The salty air always invigorated her, and the cry of the gulls was like music to her mind. But society demanded she watch from afar, safe within the confines of home.

Her father had been adamant that his daughters should be as at home on the ships as on land. And until their mother's death, they'd journeyed regularly with him. Then her aunts had stepped in, forbidding that small taste of freedom.

Elspeth sighed, focusing once more on the tableau in the drawing room.

"Should he offer, where will you reside?" Elspeth raised the question she and Isabelle had discussed the night before.

Louisa screwed her face up into a grimace. "Well, as he hasn't formally offered for me, we haven't discussed such things."

Now a frown marred Louisa's face, and Isabelle nodded at Elspeth, who drew a deep breath.

"Louisa, both Elspeth and I have thought long and hard. You'd both be welcome, if you wished, to reside here."

Elspeth glanced at Isabelle, girded her loins, then looked to her younger sister. Elspeth could no longer remain here in this house, with the constant reminder of what she would never have. A husband and children of her own. "There is plenty of room, and besides which, Isabelle and I have an interest in traveling to see the ports at which we trade and on our return, we intend to take a house in town."

Louisa's mouth dropped open, and Elspeth felt a spurt of frustration at the reaction, but that subsided when Isabelle whirled in her direction. Even as Elspeth made to step closer to her sister, to explain, the sound of feet in the hallway beyond intruded.

The door opened and their maid, Millicent, bobbed. "Mr. Lavenwood, Miss." The words were met with another tiny, bobbed curtsey, and then the black-clad woman pushed the door all the way open.

The young man entered the room, and his first glance, as always, was to Louisa before he greeted Elspeth and Isabelle.

"Mr. Lavenwood. We received your missive. You wished to talk with us?"

Jeremy Lavenwood's gaze darted around the room before returning to Louisa. He blushed deeply. "Indeed, Miss Forster. Miss Isabelle." He acknowledged them both as Elspeth moved to the large arm chair that she'd made her own.

Sinking down to the velvet padding, she waited for Jeremy to settle beside Louisa. Always the gentleman, he would never be so gauche as to take a seat before the ladies.

"Yes. That is..." He looked around. "Miss Louisa's guardian isn't here?"

Elspeth contained herself. "Our father was a trifle unusual. At our majority we came into our portions. She no longer has a guardian." Jeremy looked discomposed, but Elspeth smiled.

"Mr. Lavenwood, I promise whatever you wish to discuss will be kept within these walls." Isabelle joined the conversation for the first time, and Jeremy nodded.

"Of course, ladies. I..." He fumbled with the kerchief at the breast of his waistcoat, inhaled a ragged breath that left him trembling, then his gaze settled on Elspeth. "I wish to make an offer for Miss Louisa's hand."

Elspeth eyed the man sitting opposite.

*He's come up to scratch.*

Louisa beamed and caught her eye. For a moment, Mr. Lavenwood looked helpless, then he looked at Louisa and the worry on his face disappeared.

Taking control of the situation, Elspeth reclined further in the chair and steepled her fingers. "Mr. Lavenwood?"

His gaze jerked back in her direction.

Elspeth smiled. "By all means, let us hear your offer."

~

*T*he wedding was done. Louisa was safely wed to Mr. Lavenwood on a sunny Wednesday in May. The mad rush that had filled the house over the last several weeks had been successfully concluded, and even their aunts could find nothing to fault. With the wedding complete, the guests finally departed, and the house settled back into its usual peaceful routine.

"God, but I'm exhausted." Isabelle slumped on the chaise and fanned herself.

Elspeth knew the summer heat had sapped her sister's energy. Elspeth was glad to have divested herself of the heavy finery required to push her sister out in style, and now they were able to return to their comfortable clothes and style once more. Yet, unlike previously, when they'd successfully negotiated a major event, there was no lingering sense of satisfaction.

Isabelle broke with the rules of society, wearing her hair down. Her blonde ringlets cascaded around her shoulders and glinted in the sunlight filtering through the windows.

Elspeth breathed as deeply as possible. The forest green, silk gown and the corset beneath it were looser than the gown she'd worn earlier, yet still constricted her breathing. It hadn't stopped her slumping into her favorite winged chair. The windows were open, and the scent of the ocean breeze rushed through the house.

"At least no one will bother us now," Elspeth said.

They remained silent, two women each considering the *what next* in their lives.

"So, sister. Today we rest. Tomorrow we plan." Elspeth smiled broadly.

Isabelle's gaze turned in her direction.

"Yes, dearest. We must decide where and when."

Isabelle screeched her happiness at Elspeth's words then sobered. "What is there to plan, Elspeth? There are two ships due in the next week. They have a set route. What more discussion could there possibly be?" Isabelle's eyes now held a hint of mischief.

Elspeth nodded in agreement. She'd been considering ideas in the last three weeks, since they'd last had an opportunity to talk freely. Until now, the house had been awhirl with planning and fripperies, fittings and ordering, seating arrangements and familial visits.

"I have been thinking about your idea of traveling. We are not young ladies. We are mature. Capable. I believe the idea of visiting our trading partners is wise and appropriate." Elspeth measured every word, letting them settle in the silence between the two sisters.

Isabelle shot upright in her chair. "You mean it, Elspeth? I mean, before you intimated..."

Excitement left Isabelle glowing, and Elspeth smiled at her sister's response.

"Louisa is finally married. Settled with her husband. And once they return, they will be considering setting up a nursery. Her attention will be even more limited, while we still have our trading business to consider. Jeremy may take over running our sister's share, but to be honest, she's had little to do with the day-to-day aspects of the trade since the beginning, and I don't expect he will be interested either. That leaves us to make the decisions."

Elspeth curled her hand over the heavy, dark carving of her chair, and for a moment, she imagined the gnarled claw of her father's hand replacing the smooth knob of the seat. *You would have approved our plans, Papa.* Likely he'd even suggest which route was the most appropriate. *How I miss your presence and counsel.*

"Actually, I had even considered taking a house in town, leaving the manor for Louisa and Jeremy on our return," Elspeth said.

Isabelle bounced, clasping her hands together, then her face shadowed, and Elspeth was intrigued. "I would like to meet people, Elspeth." She spoke quietly, but with a sly smile. "We've been hidden away here since Papa died. I'd like to meet a man..." She broke off, and Elspeth jerked back in her seat.

"Indeed?" Emotions jumbled inside her. Her sister wasn't as settled to spinsterhood as she'd thought.

"Oh, Elspeth. You can't tell me that hasn't crossed your mind. What about when Sir Ludovic was here several summers ago? You found him as intriguing as most of the other women."

Indeed, he'd had a presence that had drawn women to him, like bees to the honeypot. But he'd wooed most of the young girls of the district, dashing any last hopes she'd harbored. And when he'd married... *Those thoughts are best forgotten, my girl.*

Elspeth nodded slowly. "Indeed I did. But one has to be careful in one's own town."

An idea tantalized and teased. She and her sister were now firmly on the shelf. They would become the maiden aunts to Louisa's family, but settling for a long, lonely existence made her ache. At one point she'd hoped and imagined that she too would find love. She'd wanted to marry and raise a family of her own. But now it was too late.

Her father had died and she, together with Isabelle, had taken control of Forster Shipping. She'd enjoyed the challenge, but it left her little time initially to participate in courting rituals. Then, once she'd finally had the time, her chances had come and gone. Too many years had passed.

Elspeth was no fool. Marriage wasn't for her. Not now. Perhaps she could still experience the pleasures of the flesh though. She'd heard the maids talking, and their whispers and giggles had intrigued her.

"Elspeth? I'm five and twenty. You, at seven and twenty, know that we're now too old to expect anything other than widowers looking for mothers for their children or old men. I, for one, do not envisage that kind of marriage for my future. If a spinster I must be, then I will at least have some pleasure to remember."

The mulish set of Isabelle's mouth told Elspeth her sister had set her mind to this.

Elspeth studied her sister's earnest face. Everything she'd said was correct and correlated with her own thoughts. Their future prospects were bleak.

"I too..." She looked away, embarrassed. "I have felt that." Discomfiture strangled her words, so they sounded strange even to her.

Isabelle rose and moved closer. Elspeth heard the swish of her sister's skirts on the floor. Felt the touch of Isabelle's hand on her shoulder.

"I do not wish to pass never knowing that pleasure, Elspeth."

Her stomach curled at the uncertain tone she heard in her sister's voice. Hot tears stung her eyes. *Neither do I.* She looked to the window, the sun shining brightly. Nothing had changed. Nothing ever did change. Unless she took this step, neither would she.

"You're quite right. But how?" Elspeth turned her eyes to the masts on the horizon. Inhaling deeply, she released the fear that gripped her tight. "We'll depart once Louisa and Jeremy return."

The words were power-filled. Once said, the ball of panic which had welled in her breast melted away. The clasp of Isabelle's fingers on her shoulder told her that she too felt the release.

# CHAPTER 2

*Three months later*

The air surrounding the coach had cooled overnight, and Elspeth and Isabelle shivered as they trundled down to the port. Their boxes had been sent on ahead of them in the cart last night, and all they carried was a satchel each. Their lady's maid sat opposite, her face drawn with worry.

"Miss, what if you get sick? Them heathens..."

Elspeth smiled bravely at Ellie. "That's why we have you, dear Ellie. To look after us. We'll travel on our own ship, and once in India, it will surely be easy to make enquiries and to find appropriate lodgings. After all, India is part of the empire. I have no doubt it's civilized. We'll stay for as long as it takes to conclude our business, then sail for Shanghai."

"All them bloomin' foreigners. Miss Elspeth, I won't sleep a wink 'til we's right and tight here at home."

Elspeth smothered a laugh as she adjusted her shawl over her elbows. "This is an adventure, Ellie. Come, smile for us." She herself was valiantly ignoring her own misgivings. What if they had taken on more than they could handle?

Isabelle patted Ellie's hand. "There now, dear one. All shall be as Elspeth says. We shall be safe aboard our ship and the lodgings will, no doubt, be within the fort. When I spoke to Major Fortescue's wife, she assured me that the situation is far from precarious. And Shanghai..."

The maid grumbled while Isabelle worked to charm the woman from her fearful mutterings.

Elspeth turned away from the other two, looking out the window over the green fields, letting the rocking of the carriage soothe her. She loved England, but this was likely her last opportunity to see other places. To experience adventure of the kind only men were allowed to enjoy.

The sound of the wheels rotating changed as they entered the small township, and she turned to face forward. She searched for the first sight of the masts of their clipper rising over the buildings. The *Zephyr* was a beauty of a ship. Built some twenty years before, with four tall masts and large, white sails. Her father had captained it on many long voyages during their childhood, to India and even the America's.

She and Isabelle had traveled aboard on short trips to France before their mother's death. Memories of the cramped accommodation married with feelings of well-being and excitement.

The hustle and hubbub from outside the carriage intruded on her thoughts, so she adjusted her bonnet, flicked at her skirts, and sat upright against the squabs. The teachings of her governess had sunk in well. The coach rattled to a stop at the gangway and their driver, John, hurried to open the door and put out the steps for them.

For an instant her surety faltered. She wavered.

"Elspeth?"

Her sister's call insisted she concentrate, so Elspeth blinked back her fears and rose up before descending onto the cobbles.

The coachman, who helped her down and who had been with their family for as long as she remembered, held her hand for a moment longer. "Safe travels, Miss Elspeth."

"Thank you, John. Now make sure you take the carriage home immediately. Miss Louisa and Mr. Jeremy will be needing it."

With the familiarity of time, he touched his forelock before turning back to the door. Elspeth waited for Isabelle and Ellie to alight, then they moved together. Reticules and satchels in hand, they trooped up the gangway. The wood creaked and groaned beneath their steps, but within minutes they were onboard and her gaze scoured the deck.

Captain Elliott awaited them. He was a grizzled sailing man, spare-framed with a thick beard and faded blue eyes. His hair was hidden below his customary cap, but she knew from experience that it was messy. He was both a cautious commander and a well-respected leader.

"Miss Forster, Miss Isabelle. Welcome aboard. I've cleared the captain's cabin for you both. I've also cleared Mr. Quartermaine's cabin for your maid."

Captain Elliott's first mate, Quartermaine, huddled behind the captain, but he too smiled his welcome. She'd liked him from the first moment they'd met. He was quiet but gentle, and most importantly, he had the kind of innate knowledge shared by those who had generations of ocean-traveling within their family.

"When you are ready, I'll show you the way. We've also laid in the victuals you've requested, Miss Forster." Quartermaine bowed low.

She nodded, her bonnet scratching against her neck a little. "Excellent. Then perhaps you could escort us to our cabin?"

Elspeth cast her glance over the deck. As with all their ships, it was kept in immaculate condition when at port, but she was also aware that sometimes things became a little more lax when on long voyages. Three months at sea would certainly give her the opportunity to see how the ship handled the weather and how the men responded to each other. For now, she was satisfied with the clean wood decking and appropriately attired sailors.

Quartermaine bowed again, and the three women followed him.

~

*T*he wind screamed and the *Zephyr* bucked madly, fighting for its life. The thudding on their cabin door woke Elspeth from her fitful sleep. The first she'd had in days.

"Wake up, Miss Forster!" the captain's voice called through the wood door.

She slid from the bed, making her way over the violently shuddering floor. She pulled her shawl around her shoulders and cracked the door open. The captain looked harried.

"What's wrong?" she asked.

Men scurried, their faces drawn, as she looked out into the corridor. The hanging lamps swayed from side the side, while Elspeth gripped the doorjamb.

"It's worse than I thought. You and Miss Isabelle must up and dress. Be prepared for all eventualities."

Those were words no passenger on a ship wished to hear. She stared at him. "Surely not?"

His grim visage answered her and did little to soothe her fears. "Please, you must prepare yourself."

Fear washed over her. This was supposed to be her adventure, her chance to experience life. *Is everything to end like this?*

"I'll rouse my sister."

He nodded shortly. "If we need to prepare, I'll send a man for you." Then he was gone, moving up the corridor at a rapid pace, toward the opening.

Elspeth retreated within the cabin when a thundering crack sounded. The boat shuddered again, and she screamed, launching herself at Isabelle. "Isabelle, you must wake!" She gripped her sister's shoulders and shook her.

"What?" Her sister roused. "What's going on?"

Elspeth spied the clothes they had set out earlier, before a fitful doze. The wild weather obscured any view of the sky, making it impossible to discern day from night.

"We must hurry. Captain Elliott is concerned..." She broke off, scared to say the words. "We must dress and prepare ourselves for the worst."

Her sister stared, eyes wide, and Elspeth spun away.

"Where's Ellie?" Isabelle yelled over the noise of the crashing thunder.

"In her cabin, but once we have dressed, we should go find her."

Another violent toss of the waves came, throwing her to the floor with an oomph.

"Elspeth! Elspeth, are you hurt?"

A sound, almost a scream, pierced the gloom. Her heart raced like wild horses, but the screech stopped as suddenly as it began. The ship listed a little and she spared her sister a glance.

"What do you think that was?" Elspeth shook, wrenching on stockings, hoping to ignore the reality that the *Zephyr* could sink. With quick movements, Elspeth grabbed the corset. "Here, do me up quickly, and then I'll sort you out."

Her sister stared. "But Elspeth, you aren't..."

"Hush, Isabelle. We must dress, and if that is over my night-rail, then so be it."

Her sister gave a nod and tugged on the laces. Once satisfied, Elspeth encouraged Isabelle to tie them off, before she reached for Isabelle's. Elspeth held tight and pulled. Finally satisfied, she hurried to struggle into her gown.

"Oh, Elspeth, I fear something has happened to Ellie. Otherwise, she'd be here with us."

She too felt that in the pit of her stomach and nodded with a jerk. "Grab your life preserver and we'll go check on her."

Another thud and a scream echoed, and this time Isabelle clutched at her hand. "That sounded like..."

Her stomach cramped further. During the day the storm had grown in intensity, the seas violent and boiling beneath the prow of the ship, and her disquiet had grown. Now fear held her in its iron grip.

"Put your preserver on, Isabelle." She struggled into hers, hearing the cries from the deck.

Suddenly, the boat righted once more, throwing them to the door. Elspeth gripped the knob and turned the metal hard. Together the two sisters fell into the corridor.

They groped their way to the first mate's cabin and opened the door. Elspeth gasped, her eyes taking in the sight before her.

On the floor she saw a pair of feet, the rest of the body hidden by a large traveling trunk. *Her* trunk. She surged forward, but already knew.

"Ellie!" Isabelle screamed from the door.

Elspeth didn't waste a moment, dropping to the floor to pull the trunk to the side. The cracked and faded leather creaked and groaned but wouldn't move.

"We're going to need help." She looked around at Isabelle, trying to banish the memory of the hideous truth she'd spied in the cabin. Elspeth waited for a reaction from her white-faced sister.

"Ellie..."

"I think she's dead, Isabelle."

Her sister's face crumpled as she began to cry.

"Come. We should go back to our cabin." Elspeth rose unsteadily and lurched back toward her sister.

"But Ellie?"

"There's nothing we can do. The men are working to save the ship. Once that is done, then we will seek their aid."

It felt wrong to leave Ellie there, yet she had herself and her sister to consider first. Right now, Isabelle, the ship, and the crew were her priority. So she shut the door behind her and towed the sobbing woman in her arms back to their cabin.

Elspeth sat waiting, the cork vest chafing at her through the layers of the hastily donned gown for what felt like hours. She barely dared to move, as if her actions might be the last insult to the ship. Instead, she gripped Isabelle's hand, and they huddled together, waiting for the call to abandon ship.

Elspeth listened to the thuds, creaks, and groans of the ailing vessel, fighting the fury of nature, every sound jolting her system like a blow. Gradually, the raging wind, rain, and lightning lessened—petered away—and she drowsed, upright in the bunk where she had her head resting against her sister's shoulder.

The sound of footsteps woke her. She looked around to see that the glow of daylight shone through the tiny window. "Wake up, Isabelle!" She pushed at her sister.

Isabelle opened her eyes. "Do we have to..."

Elspeth shuddered. "Isabelle? I think we survived the night."

A knock came at the door. "Miss Forster? Miss Isabelle?"

She slid off the bunk and made her way to the door, straightening her rumpled gown as best she could.

The captain, his face more grizzled and more tired than she'd ever seen before, waited on the other side. "We have survived. But..."

There was nothing to be gained from prodding the man who obviously was both tired and emotionally strained, so she waited.

"We lost two men last night, and one... He'll not recover."

For the first time she heard the faint sounds, which must have come from down below. They weren't screams so much as groans of pain.

"Is there nothing we can do?" she asked.

Captain Elliott shook his head. "No."

She breathed deeply. "Our maid, in the first mate's cabin...she didn't survive either."

He nodded. "My men will attend to her then."

"Thank you, Captain."

He turned away and she drew back into the cabin, shutting

the door.

~

"Three months, two weeks, and six days." Elspeth rose
and walked slowly to the small window.

"I for one cannot wait to be back on land." Isabelle was a
mere ghost of herself, her voice faint and languid. Elspeth cast a
glance at her sister Isabelle, who was resting on the bed.

"Yes. I too."

The voyage had been more than trying, first with the storm
and the loss of Ellie. Elspeth still couldn't believe she was gone,
crushed beneath the trunk that had worked itself free of the
securing straps that were meant to hold the item in place.

They'd also lost crewmembers that night. One of the men had
been struck by the mast as it snapped in the gale force winds.
He'd been tossed overboard. Another had been caught in the
riggings, and as fast as they had worked to cut them away, he had
still perished. A third had taken spars from the mast in his
midsection. With no physician aboard, his death had been slow
and terrible. He'd cried and moaned until the silence descended.
The memories of the white-shrouded bodies slipping over the
side of the ship left her chilled.

Elspeth rubbed her arms, seeking warmth, though the
weather now was humid.

In the last week Isabelle had fallen ill. Pale and listless, she
coughed regularly, a dry and racking sound. Captain Elliott
suggested making landfall in Bombay. Isabelle though had
demurred, urging them to make for their destination with all
speed, but food stocks were low. Elspeth kept a close eye on her
sister, constantly evaluating the situation. She now agreed with
Captain Elliott—Bombay was their best chance.

"Did you enjoy the Suez Canal, dearest? The land around is
so different to England."

They had passed out of the Red Sea a week or more ago. The trip was coming to an end. Soon they would make landfall in Bombay, replenish the ship's stocks, then they would begin the final leg to Calcutta.

Isabelle nodded slowly. "Oh yes, that was so interesting. To see the gates working was such a marvel." She brushed a pale lock from her forehead.

Elspeth noted the sheen of sweat on her skin. The temperature wasn't so hot yet, so that surely wasn't the reason for the dampness of Isabelle's skin.

"I'm pleased we are almost there," Isabelle said.

"Are you hot?" Elspeth was worrief?

"Not really. You should rest, Elspeth. You have been running after me for what feels like an age."

Elspeth shook her gown, wishing she could remove the her concerns as easily. "Isabelle, I can't sit." She made her way around the room again, setting everything to rights, then scooped up another gown, looking critically for any tears or stains. "Soon we will be in Bombay, then we shall summon a physician."

Isabelle turned away, and Elspeth felt a pang. They needed to get to Calcutta, but if Isabelle were truly sick with malaria, they couldn't afford not to seek the assistance of a doctor. She bit her lip, worrying over the decisions she'd made. Responsibility weighed heavily.

Isabelle coughed again, her entire body shaking, and Elspeth felt a spurt of anguish. "I'm going to see the captain. I want to make sure he understands that on landfall your health is our first priority. I'm just thankful we'll arrive in the next day or two."

Her sister didn't answer, didn't so much as sigh. Heavy though it was, some of the tension in Isabelle's body looked to have seeped away.

"Will you be fine if I go see the captain?"

"Go."

The muffled word defeated Elspeth, and her shoulders

slumped. She placed the gown down on the bed and pulled on light, lacy gloves before gripping the parasol and heading through the wooden doors. Once in the corridor she strode out onto the deck, thankful for the small coverage afforded her in the burning heat as she made her way to the bridge.

"Miss Forster! Glad to see you. I do hope your sister is feeling improved?"

Elspeth just shook her head, and Captain Elliott frowned.

"I see," he said.

Quartermaine rounded the corner. "You're just in time, Miss Forster. We should be sighting land anytime now."

"So soon? I thought..." Her words trailed away as the captain grinned at her.

"We've made excellent time."

Turning and looking in the direction the captain pointed to, Elspeth spotted a flat horizon. There wasn't yet much to see, but even as she squinted a cry came from the crow's nest above.

"Land ho!"

Excitement sparked inside her, and she leaned closer to the railing, straining. She noted a shimmer on the surface of the ocean, and the longer she stared the more detail became obvious. Now sails dotted the horizon.

The captain pulled the scope out, the snap loud in the sudden silence, and gazed forward.

"How long, Captain?"

"Not long. Several hours, I would presume, Miss Elspeth."

"Excellent." With that Elspeth returned below decks.

~

*E*lspeth looked down on the hubbub from the railing of the *Zephyr*, watching as Quartermaine disappeared into the boiling mass of humanity of the wharf. Women and men in strange, bright clothing moved rapidly here and there. The bay too was busy with ships loading and offloading cargo, the lowing of cattle matching the cacophony of cries on the dock. There was also a contingent of marines, their rifles gripped tightly. She'd enquired why they were needed, and the captain's face had tightened.

"Riots, Miss Forster. They tried to gain control of the areas outside of Bombay and in the interior, but our troops dealt with the insurrection."

"They didn't get into Bombay then?"

"Not this time."

Her hands gripped the oiled wood as she ate up the scene unfolding before her. She noted the turbaned men, their pale pants and slipper-like shoes, and the women with brightly covered scarves and long gowns. Every now and again one would look up, their face tight and vicious, and she'd draw away from the side.

Footsteps heralded the captain moving close alongside her. "Some women assume western garb, while others remain in the traditional saree."

She quirked an eyebrow at Captain Elliott, but he moved away, leaving her alone once more. She turned back, noting the gentlemen and soldiers who strolled among the masses, curling moustaches and uniforms standing out like drab herons among the colorful parade.

The city beyond beckoned, but she remained resolute at the rail, taking in as much as she could of the town from her view. The white buildings in the distance and lining the foreshore, so alien in design, caught her eyes. Rounded rooflines married with the gothic columns. Bombay was not a city that they had time to explore, and according to the harbor master, it wasn't safe.

This port was merely a short stop to seek medical assistance and replenish their supplies enough to see them through to their ultimate destination. Captain Elliott had cautioned her against leaving the ship, so she hadn't even ventured down the gangplank. It went against all her instincts to refrain from exploring this foreign land, but it was far too dangerous for a white *memsahib* to venture ashore alone, and because of the precious cargo of seed they carried, the ship required guarding. It would remain that way until they set sail once more.

Her need to traverse and inspect would be neither useful nor a businesslike decision, she silently admitted. So, she waited for Quartermaine to return with a physician in tow.

"Oh, Isabelle, if only you could see this." Her sister remained holed up in their cabin, too ill to leave her bunk.

The scent of spices filled the air, and she breathed deeply, her senses welcoming the redolent smells. She tugged at her collar, the closely heated dampness making her skin itch in the humid air. Elspeth raised her head and noted the heavy, black clouds rolling in.

*When we reach Calcutta I shall have new gowns, suitable for the weather, made up for both of us.* Maybe she'd even instruct the seamstress to furnish her with a saree, she thought with a smile.

Within an hour, Quartermaine returned, bounding up the gangplank, while their seamen loaded the necessary supplies the captain had ordered. He was followed by two men and a woman. The older gentleman was mopping his face with a cloth, his face red with exertion. She could easily pick the doctor, and watched the stony-faced woman who accompanied him.

Her gaze ranged over the newcomers and settled on the younger man beside the doctor.

*Who is the other man with Quartermaine?* He was tall. Muscular, if the fit of his jacket was anything to go by, with a strong jaw and piercing gray eyes. There was an indefinable quality about him. The presence drew her gaze, holding it prisoner.

The doctor in a severe black suit queried Isabelle's illness and snapped her back to reality. "What symptoms does my patient exhibit?"

She stepped forward. "Doctor? If you would follow me, I'll

take you to my sister."

The physician smiled at her, kindly, she thought. He was well-rounded with a rather large moustache, curled at the end. His dark hair was cut quite short against his scalp, probably because of the heat, she imagined.

"I have brought Mrs. Ellington with me. She acts as my nurse."

The woman smiled, and Elspeth realized she wasn't as old as her first impression had given. Perhaps in her third decade she'd surmised, but now, on closer inspection, she would guess younger than that. Being dressed in the heavy black of mourning aged her.

"How do you do? Doctor, Mrs. Ellington, if you'll follow me." She moved quickly across the deck, leading the way. "My sister has been running fevers, exhibiting a dry cough. The captain..." She stopped her words, swallowing the dread. "The captain fears it could be malaria."

They clattered down the tiny stairs and headed directly to the cabin. As Elspeth pushed the door back, she could see the concern on the doctor's face, feeding the terror which had lodged within her chest. *So many illnesses are fatal.* Elspeth banished the thought with difficulty. She closed the door, hanging back while the doctor and Mrs. Ellington consulted with Isabelle. The entire time, she bunched her fingers together, trying to be positive about the situation.

Eventually, with a grunt, the doctor turned back. "In my considered opinion, Miss Isabelle does indeed have malaria."

She gasped, unable to contain the single sound of panic. "What... What can we do?" The captain's words hovered at the edges of her consciousness. Many died from malaria. *I can't lose Isabelle.* She fought and controlled the panic again.

"Come, Miss Forster. Let us go up top, and I can explain the treatment while Mrs. Ellington makes your sister more comfortable."

She followed the doctor back up the corridor and out into the sun.

"Your sister is lucky in that she has only been ill a short period of time, according to Mr. Quartermaine. But let me be blunt. She requires rest and nursing. Also she will require regular doses of quinine."

Elspeth frowned. "But... Will she be able to travel? We must reach Calcutta, as we have urgently required cargo."

The doctor harrumphed. "The tonic Mrs. Ellington is administering will help. It's quinine-based. The most effective tonic available, and is under patent to the Admiralty. But it's no good without all the other precautions in place. To be quite frank, Miss Forster, I would feel better if she were in the infirmary here. Under a physician's direction."

Elspeth worried her lip as she considered his words. "What kind of precautions?" She looked into the doctor's face. "We really can't afford to wait, and from the looks of those clouds, we won't have much time here." The need to consider and decide weighed heavily on her mind.

He nodded. "I understand. Keep her quiet. Treat her symptoms as usual, plenty of cool, damp cloths and water. Soft foods would be best, and bed rest. Will you be able to cope with that, Miss Forster? Or will you require a nurse?"

She turned away as doubts and fears assailed her. Would it be better to have a nurse on hand? It would be one more body aboard the ship. After the loss of Ellie, Elspeth wasn't sure she wanted to be responsible for another soul, yet on the other hand, another woman aboard would be useful...and welcome. *Someone to talk to.*

"Do you know of someone?" The sound of footsteps behind her caught Elspeth's attention.

"Miss Forster? I'm looking to return to England now that I have nothing to keep me here."

She turned in the direction of the dour Mrs. Ellington.

"I would be more than happy to nurse your sister, especially if...."

Elspeth blinked rapidly, letting her mind turn over the situation.

"Doctor? Are you able to release Mrs. Ellington? We can ensure that she reaches England aboard our ship." She gnawed at her lip as the doctor's mouth flattened. It seemed that he was unhappy to be losing his nurse. "And my sister would have adequate and skilled care. We would even compensate you and Mrs. Ellington." She hoped to sweeten the deal with funds, so they could swiftly seal the agreement.

"Then I must concede. She will be in no more danger aboard the ship than she would be here. In fact, possibly even better cared for. Your journey won't be long, and there are more physicians and better facilities in Calcutta." He sighed. "But you have stolen away my best nurse."

Elspeth nodded at his words then turned to see Mrs. Ellington hovering. "I need to check with the captain, but I don't see..." Another thought intruded. "Your family?"

"My husband's dead. I can be ready very quickly, Miss Forster. We... *I* do not have many items to take home with me."

"You said *we*?"

"My lately departed husband and I. It's hard to remember he is now gone."

"I understand losing someone close, Mrs. Ellington." And she did, after the loss of both

her parents. "I would need you to remain in Calcutta with my sister while she is ill. It could be some time before I can send you to England as we will need to wait for the return of one of our vessels. The *Zephyr* will be making its return journey as soon as we disembark and the outgoing cargo is loaded."

"I understand that, Miss Forster. My family is... My son and daughter are in England at school, so there would be no concerns on that front. I want to go home, but cannot..."

Understanding bloomed. She had no money to pay for her passage home. Elspeth laid her hand on the woman's arm. "One moment then, while I discuss this with the captain." She might be the owner of the shipping line, but all such queries needed to be directed to him.

A quick glance showed him in deep discussion by the gangway. She hurried over to him, fanning herself slightly under the heat of the noonday sun.

"Captain?"

"Yes, Miss Forster?" He turned, looking harried and more than a little tense.

"Captain, the doctor has made a diagnosis of malaria. I have explained that we are unable to remain in Bombay. He has a nurse however. I should like for her to join us until we reach our destination in Calcutta, then to remain with my sister until such time as my sister is well again."

He frowned, his two bushy eyebrows almost merging as he ran his fingers through his beard, a thoughtful expression on his face. "Well, Mr. Quartermaine? Where would we put the nurse?"

"I thought she would take the cabin next door? Is that no longer acceptable?" She noted the telltale blush on Quartermaine's face; clearly he had news to impart that didn't sit well with his view of how things should be.

"Well, you see Miss Forster, the other gentleman who came on at the same time as the doctor, he's with the army. They need us to get him to Calcutta with all due speed."

"In other words, Miss Forster, he has commandeered us to carry him to Calcutta. Quartermaine has already had to explain that he will need to use that cabin, because he demanded the captain's, but you are using it."

"Then where would..." She stopped fanning her face as the information sank in.

"She would have to share your cabin."

# CHAPTER 3

*a*eddan watched the woman as she glided across the deck. The overhang shadows he waited in afforded him an excellent view without being seen. She couldn't know that he watched her.

The woman was lush, curved in all the right places, and the molded bodice of cream silk enhanced her assets nicely. *My, what bountiful assets she has too.* Her tightly coiled hair accentuated the swanlike lines of her neck, and her skin glowed. She was perfectly comfortable with sea-going. *What an exotic creature.*

Quartermaine strode in his direction. "That's Miss Forster. She and her sister, Miss Isabelle, are owners of the company. She's a looker, ain't she? She's also a lady."

He understood the implicit warning in the other man's words. *Hands off.*

Such a shame. *Miss Forster. Unmarried.* He smiled. Maybe some small dalliance would be welcome. He'd seen the look she cast his way. The interest she'd advertised in her gaze when he'd come aboard.

She turned from the rail and headed back below. Her movements were graceful, and he let himself watch, mesmerized.

"Major?" Quartermaine interrupted his thoughts.

"Indeed? And Miss Isabelle?" Aeddan looked out of the masses milling on the wharf, the hurly-burly of trade, looking for his batman. Surely Grundy wasn't taking this long to retrieve their bags from the place where they had lodged overnight?

"Miss Isabelle is sick, Major. She's got malaria."

He looked back at Quartermaine with a frown. "And they are not sending her to the infirmary?"

Quartermaine shook his head, a small frown between his eyes, the leathery skin creasing slightly. "No, sir. Instead, they are taking on a nurse. She's to help with Miss Isabelle. Save Miss Forster some worry. Let her rest."

He grunted, considering Quartermaine's words. Malaria was certainly treatable, but for a lady, gently reared... "She is the owner, you say?"

"Aye, she is, Major. She and Miss Isabelle have run the company since the death of their father. Built it up over the years. This trip she will be looking at the suppliers. Seeing what new opportunities there are for Forster Shipping. The Cap'n thinks she might also be considering newer, faster ships." The man's voice rasped, a common trait in career seamen.

In his three decades, he'd rarely seen a woman employed in business, and those that were, he'd always found rough. Hardened by the day-to-day act of trading and mercantile. In Miss Forster, he'd seen none of that. And yet, it seemed, she was involved and in charge of ensuring this small line was successful.

"Family?" He moved closer to the gangway, and Quartermaine followed him.

"Only one other sister, Miss Louisa, who has recently wed into the gentry."

The more he heard about Miss Forster, the more intrigued he became. In his mind's eye rose a vision; red hair piled high, shining green eyes beckoning, twinkling with laughter. He saw a softly rounded face of healthy womanhood, slightly tanned but firm skin, with dips and curves that caught his attention. He blinked as his body reacted to his thoughts.

So many questions he wanted to ask. He tamped them down. All in good time. He wasn't Viceroy Hasting's top spy for nothing. He'd learned the value of waiting and watching. Of engineering circumstances as needed.

He glanced over Quartermaine's shoulder to see a man hurrying, valise tugged tight against his chest, and the crowd parting for him. He made the ship, scurried up the gangplank, then blinked and turned, unerringly in Aeddan's direction.

"Ah, here's Grundy now. Would you show us to my cabin? And I will need another for my man."

Quartermaine shook his head, his face clearly displaying his discomfort. "I'm sorry, Major, there ain't no more. Miss Forster and Miss Isabelle will be sharing with Mrs. Ellington. You and your man will have the smaller cabin. That's all there is. Miss Forster is already using the ready room as her office and dining room and we use it for bunking down."

Such arrangements didn't really suit him at all, to be stuck in some pokey little cabin. Alfred Grundy snored. It would be a long week, or however long this trip would take. He'd have to suffer the noise and likely toss and turn. But he'd have to accept the situation.

Grundy approached. "I got it all, Major. Sold the horses as you instructed too."

"Very good, Grundy. We'll be sailing..." He turned to Quartermaine, raising an eyebrow.

"When all is settled for Miss Isabelle, Major. Shouldn't be long though. The ladies understand the tides. Ocean's in their blood, see? Right proper ladies they are."

He smiled to himself. *Indeed, Miss Forster is a right proper lady.*

∾

*I*sabelle, I am so pleased you feel a little improved." Elspeth smiled as her sister dressed, for the first time in weeks, in a light blue tea gown of brushed cotton. The dress hung loosely on Isabelle's frame, leaving her looking pale yet interesting. Her blonde hair, so like their late mother's, hung in a long plait down her back.

"Mrs. Ellington has done wonders for me. But I should like to see the ocean again."

Elspeth had to strain to hear Isabelle's voice, still quiet as she recovered. Elspeth moved behind her sister, quickly unfastening the ribbon in Isabelle's hair, and ran her brush in long sweeps through the heavy tresses. "The air will do you wonders, I'm sure, and put some color in your cheeks."

The small mirror in Isabelle's hand wavered for a moment, and Elspeth caught sight of herself. Her own skin was no longer white, as was fashionable, but lightly tinted a golden honey tone.

"You said we have new passengers? Tell me about them," Isabelle begged.

"Uh, there is Major Fitzsimmons. A nice-looking gentleman. He is traveling with his man, Grundy."

She tried to avoid Isabelle's question, deftly twisting her sister's hair into an elegant if plainly coiled bun at her nape. Indeed, Major Fitzsimmons was far more than just a nice-looking gentleman. Since catching sight of him, her mind wanted to weave impossible fantasies.

He was muscular, she'd already seen that. With gray eyes and a chiseled jaw, he was every woman's dream consort. He possessed a lock of black hair that teased her senses, and when carelessly arranged, it would dance in the sea breeze.

"Now that we have found our parasols we are ready to call Quartermaine to have you carried up top."

"Oh, Elspeth, I'm sure I can manage."

"Nonsense, Isabelle. Mrs. Ellington says you must not exert yourself." Elspeth hurried to the door, opening it.

She almost swallowed her tongue, as on the other side of the door stood Major Fitzsimmons. His presence was commanding. He made her feel small. Not petite, no man alive could do that, she thought with uncommon whimsy—she was too tall to achieve that dubious honor—but feminine.

"May I help you, Miss Forster?" He bowed and that lock of black hair flicked forward, catching her attention. When he righted himself, his eyes gazed into hers. Her chest seized, as if her very breath were stolen.

"I was about to call for Quartermaine. My sister will need to be conveyed topside." Her hands fluttered toward the cabin door.

"Then allow me."

Before she could demur, he moved within, making a bow to her sister, who smiled prettily.

"Miss Isabelle, I presume? I am Major Fitzsimmons, and I'm at your command. I have stolen from Mr. Quartermaine the privilege of carrying you above, fair lady."

Isabelle laughed. "Good morning, Major Fitzsimmons."

Elspeth grit her teeth at the humor in her sister's voice.

An uneasy emotion wormed its way through Elspeth. One she had no intention of considering, otherwise she was sure she'd find it lacking in grace. Instead, she picked up the other parasol which lay on her makeshift bed.

As Major Fitzsimmons gathered up her sister, she caught a hint of rippling muscles beneath his white shirt. Not for the first time since catching sight of him, she wondered about the man. Here was no pampered officer, yet he had courtly manners and was well-spoken. There were no rough edges to him.

Elspeth trailed them out, closing the door before ascending the stairs leading to the deck and into the sunshine. Mrs. Ellington waited for them, chairs in place and shawls at the ready. Elspeth shaded her eyes, looking out over the ocean as the major settled her sister in the rattan chair they'd taken onboard in Bombay.

"Captain Elliott tells me we should arrive in Calcutta in another two days, Miss Forster. I'm sure you and your sister will be pleased to be back on dry land."

She turned, startled by his words. "Indeed, this has been an extraordinarily long voyage. For both myself and my sister."

"Would you..." He indicated the length of the deck. "...take a turn with me?"

Casting a quick glance at her sister, she bit her lip. She felt torn by his request. It meant time alone with this virile man who made her feel quite off-balance. On the other hand, she surely should look to the interests of Isabelle. A glance at Isabelle showed her reclined in a chair with eager eyes scanning the horizon. Mrs. Ellington had taken the seat beside her, and engaged her quickly in some deep conversation.

She frowned, feeling quite unnecessary. In a fit of pique, she turned to the major with a smile. "I... Yes. I'd like that, very much."

He smiled and the softening of his features, usually so firm and sharp, gave way to the crinkling at his eyes. The look melted an area hidden deep within her chest in the region of her heart. He took her hand, the touch careful. Everything about his manner was correct, yet there was something intimate in the way he placed her hand on his arm.

With slow deliberation he began the promenade, and she moved with him, their bodies traveling in a smooth and synchronous fashion.

"How long do you plan to stay in Calcutta?" he asked.

She focused on the view ahead, the expanse of ocean a vista of blue. "I should think we shall be there for perhaps upward of a year."

Her footsteps were muffled by the sounds of men moving like well-oiled machines, in the rigging above her or mending sails.

"What could possibly entice you to stay for that long, Miss Forster?" He stopped her, one hand firmly grasping hers. The shock and surprise in both his tone and on his face took her aback.

"I have business to conduct. Merchants to meet with, and I should like to see where the cloth and spices we import are obtained from."

He looked startled at her answer before the emotion was hidden away from view. "Miss Forster, that's a man's occupation. Not for such a female as yourself."

Clear in his tone was a lack of understanding of how vital this mission was, not just to Forster Shipping but also for her personally. Anger and ridiculous disappointment churned, while a deep well of unrelieved frustration arose at the thought of the barriers her gender constantly met.

"Sir, I am more than capable—"

"That is not what I meant." His tone turned conciliatory, as if realizing he'd slighted her, but she held herself stiff. "You are a lady. Learned, but still a woman. It is unsafe for you to..."

"Major Fitzsimmons, excuse me, but I daresay that glib tongue of yours no doubt weaves a silken thread when required. To me, it is naught but a net. The net that has caught those of my sex for years. Stopped us from participating in trade and economic undertakings which would allow us to feed and clothe families without the need for a man. I am as able as—"

"Damn it, for all that though, you are a woman." His cheeks glowed, and his eyes glittered like hard, cold stones.

His words stilled her. "I am." She inclined her head. "But that does not—"

"This is no tame drawing room you are entering. It is a society that lives and breathes patriarchy. The men will treat you with disdain, which is *if* they will see you. Did you not seek information before setting off on this harebrained scheme of yours?"

A hot spurt of anger coursed at his words, but a tiny seed of doubt also rose. "I beg your pardon, Major, but perhaps you should return me to my sister now." She attempted to pull free, but he held her hand tightly.

"Wait. I should not have spoken so candidly or baldly." With his hand clasped over hers, she had no choice but to stay and hear his words. "Indeed, I spoke out of turn. I am concerned that you and your sister may be putting yourself in danger without having made adequate arrangements for a male to guide you."

"I believe then, that you jumped to a conclusion. I sent a telegraph while in Bombay to my agent in Calcutta. He will act for me and arrange satisfactory accommodation. He will look to Mrs. Ellington's return home as well. I am neither alone nor friendless."

"Forgive me then, Miss Forster. I did not wish to imply that you were unable to arrange such necessary chaperonage."

He'd drawn her into the shade, the overhang from the small room at the bow of the ship affording them some privacy. Elspeth was grateful to be out of sight of the prying eyes of the sailors. She took a moment to compose herself before speaking again.

"Sir, let me tell you once—were I a man, your comments would have resulted in more than the sharp edge of my tongue."

"And so I should expect. Forgive me, Miss Forster. *Pax*?"

She looked at him, noting the smile curling around those enticing lips of his, his eyes hooding slightly. Delicious heat once more curled in her belly, but this time it wasn't the heat of anger. The heat spread a languor through her body.

"Yes, of course, Major." She couldn't contain the breathless whisper, and he crowded in. She stepped back, unwilling to allow any close contact. In her mind, consciousness whispered that way led to danger.

～

*A*eddan knew the moment awareness impinged on the delightful Miss Forster. It was clear in the way her eyes widened, her face flushed, and she stepped back from him. He couldn't control his impulse and followed her, seeking some small contact.

A stray red strand escaped from the intricate coil of her hair, and he reached forward, touching the silken thread with his fingers. "So soft."

His awareness centered on her. He tucked the errant curl behind her ear. She vibrated at his touch, and her pink lips parted.

He moved closer, needing to kiss her. Feel the whispering caress of her breath against him. He was a sensualist. He'd accepted that knowledge long ago, had fed it during the years he'd been in India, but never had he wanted that connection with such force, either sexual or of any other variety, until now.

Now fervor drove him mercilessly. Demanding he assuage the pit of need that grew inside his gut.

She intrigued him on a level he'd never before experienced. What was it about this woman that she lured him like a siren? He wanted to touch her. He hungered to please her. To taste the warm, fragrant cavern of her mouth, so that he might know more of her. Frustration ate at him, a savage hunger demanding fulfillment.

"I must..." She swayed toward him, the fingers of one of her hands touching his chest, burning him where they fluttered.

He leaned in, giving himself to the momentary pleasure of touching his lips against hers. They were soft. Warm and plump.

With great care, he sipped at the fullness he'd found, tasting the very essence of her breath. His hands wound their way around her back as she leaned in. He held her still as she moaned slightly, her body loosening in his caress.

"'Round 'ere boys. Cap'n wants us to wash the decks." The

cant words of the sailors intruded on him. They wafted from the other side of their dubious screen.

Aeddan pulled back, letting go of her. At some point in the embrace her eyes had closed, and she opened them now, blinking owlishly. Her face flushed then her mouth opened in an 'o'.

"How... How dare you?" Her eyes flashed like shining emeralds as she hurried to straighten her hair, which had been disarrayed during the embrace.

"Miss Forster, I do beg your pardon." He bowed, hiding the tiny grin he fought to control. When he straightened he saw the way her lips tightened, lines of white bracketing her lush mouth.

"I shall return to my sister now."

She projected a don't-touch-me air he found challenging, and his mind dealt with the many ways he could change her attitude. Bring her to heel. Then reality intruded and reminded him that he'd pushed as far as he dared. For now.

"Of course." He offered his arm, and she looked at him, disdain clear in the way her eyes challenged him.

"I think not, sir." With a swish of her skirts, she moved, gliding across the deck and around the building before disappearing from his sight.

He waited, cooling his overheated body before following her.

# CHAPTER 4

*T*he meal passed in a companionable manner, and Aeddan found himself looking at Miss Isabelle in the lamplight. As tempting as many men might find her, she couldn't hold a candle to her sister's shining beauty.

Even as the light picked up the silvery tones in the strands of Isabelle's hair, it was the fiery titian with red and gold that roused him. He didn't question his attraction to her, or just where it would take him.

"Sir, you have been most secretive about your position in India. We know you hold the position of Major, but with which brigade?" Mrs. Ellington, a faded matron who looked to be in her third decade, addressed him.

He looked at her, taking in the tightly scraped back, black hair and the outmoded gown of black cotton. She reminded him of a crow beside the two jeweled beauties who joined them at the table. But she was good-natured, and an excellent nurse-companion for Miss Isabelle.

"Mrs. Ellington, until recently I have been with the Royal Artillery, but am to be redeployed on my arrival in Calcutta." He was taking a chance telling them this much, but he was going to be in a fix if he couldn't tell them which regiment. He made a mental note to inform Grundy and spread the word through the ranks on arrival.

The others at the table continued discussing the current state of affairs in India. Miss Forster looked down at the empty plate.

He waited as the cook's boy cleared them away, pouring himself another drink from the decanter, then indicated toward her and she looked up with a nod. He refilled her glass and sat back, studying her. The burnished gown accenting the slight tan of her skin gave her the look of an avenging goddess.

"Indeed, Major, so you have been in India for some time?"

Miss Forster was watching him, her face shuttered, and he wanted to sigh. He'd scared her earlier with his advances. While he sensed a deep well of passion in her, she was an English gentlewoman. She would need time to accept him. He'd settled on her in his mind as the perfect consort, and the thrill of the chase rippled through his body. Awareness flooded him the first time he'd seen her, and that intensity continued to grow, like a conflagration banked just before it roared into life.

He nodded. "Yes, several years."

Miss Forster fiddled with her napkin, obviously uncertain. "We have heard tales of men bringing back Indian ways when they return to England."

She glanced under her eyelashes at him. Teasing him. For an instant surprise flared, then he felt a smile inching across his face.

*The tigress has claws.*

"Miss Forster, India is a land with many things to recommend it. Perhaps after you have been there a while, you might tell me what you have found the most intriguing?"

She looked away, and the loss of her gaze signaled the end of their private repartee.

"I... Uh. My sister has been unwell again today. I do hope it isn't a relapse." Her words were muffled, and he frowned in Miss

Isabelle's direction. She touched Miss Forster's hand, as if attempting to reassure her.

"Elspeth, I am sure I will be well by the time we make landfall." Clearly, these two women had a close relationship, and the illness of the younger sister concerned him.

"Perhaps when we make landfall, you might visit the infirmary? There are many well-respected physicians there." He hoped she would. He'd seen the ravages of malaria firsthand, and he would hate to see it take its toll on Isabelle.

Miss Forster—Elspeth—cast him a grateful glance. The look warmed him.

"I have been telling Isabelle that since we left Bombay."

Isabelle did look pale. Beads of moisture formed on her face, and he frowned.

Elspeth must have spied it too as she laid her napkin on the table. "If you will excuse us? I had best see my sister to rest. Gentlemen, thank you for an interesting night."

He nodded, then as the senior lady of the group, she rose and the others followed suit. She smiled faintly, and for a moment her eyes rested on him. He returned her gaze, watching for her reaction. Then Elspeth glanced away and left the room.

A faint scent of English rose wafted in the air, and he inhaled deeply, realizing it was the same scent he'd smelled on her outside, during the day...during their encounter. He savored the essence before his thoughts were interrupted by the captain placing a decanter before him.

"Major, will you have another port and share what you know of the unrest between the government and the Amir?"

He leaned back, uncomfortably aware that though the question was innocent, his knowledge of the situation was far more detailed than he could share. "I have heard that an envoy was sent to Sher Ali Khan. The envoy was refused. Turned back."

Captain Elliott looked scandalized. "Surely not? That would lead to..."

"Indeed, there are those who are already saying that in Bombay."

In truth he knew that Lord Lytton had sent Neville Chamberlain to meet with the Sher in the full knowledge that the mission would be turned away. He, himself, had also been directed to act as a covert viewer of the Afghani machinations. His location secured well before the Russian envoys had arrived in Kabul.

With his report written immediately after viewing the meeting, he'd hurried back to Bombay with information of the Amir's wish to keep Afghanistan neutral in the unstable political climate.

The travel had been arduous, twenty days on horseback and a further ten by rail, but he'd had to stay ahead of anyone tracking him. He couldn't even use the dubious speed of the electric telegraph as the information he carried was too important. If it was intercepted by anyone, their advantage would be lost. Everything he did would strengthen the position of the empire.

"The information that the mission was denied was transported via telegraph. Apart from that..." He shrugged. *Let them draw their own conclusions.*

A rap came at the door, and the captain gave the command to enter. Quartermaine hurried in. "Captain, Miss Isabelle has taken a turn. Miss Forster thought you should know."

~

*I*sabelle lay still on the bed, Elspeth eying her with increasing concern. In the last few days since Isabelle collapsed after the dinner, she'd castigated herself. She and Mrs. Ellington had been nursing her in shifts. Now she was waiting for the other woman to take over and allow her a break.

The bubble of worry consumed her, tearing at her mind. The cabin had somehow become her prison, and she hated it. Hated being on the ship and powerless. The vagaries of female emotions had never before assailed her. Now she vacillated and second-guessed her every action. All the while the thought ate at her *did I do the right thing by agreeing to this adventure?* The loss of Ellie had been a blow, but to lose Isabelle...

The door of the cabin opened and she heard the swish of skirts on the planking. "Miss Forster, go up top for a while. Take some air and rest. We'll be fine here."

Elspeth turned grateful eyes on Mrs. Ellington. "You're sure?"

The question was rhetorical. She knew she needed to escape from the confinement of the small cabin.

At Mrs. Ellington's nod, she sighed. "Just for a while then." She quickly grabbed her gloves and parasol from the small table in the center and headed for the door. "Call me if..."

"I will. But I doubt we will need to call you. Now go. Shoo!"

The door opened and she trudged out, not paying attention. "Oomph!" She connected with a hard chest, and strong hands caught her. A tingle rippled through her body.

Looking up, Elspeth glanced into Major Fitzsimmons's eyes. The momentary concern for her sister disappeared, replaced by something of an equally concerning nature—the confusion of emotions she experienced around this man.

"Oh, I do beg your pardon. I wasn't..."

"All is well, Miss Elspeth?"

She frowned at his use of her name while an odd sense of vertigo assailed her. Emotions welled and ebbed, leaving her light-headed for just a moment, before that too fled.

"Yes, thank you, Major. I was going up top to take some air." Her voice sounded breathless, as if she couldn't control even that most basic function.

"Then take my arm and I will join you." His hands fell away, and for a moment loss flooded her, only to be replaced with calmness as he slid her arm through his. "Your sister?"

"There is little change. Mrs. Ellington and I are worried.

When we make landfall tomorrow she will be transferred immediately to the infirmary."

"Yes, that would be the best thing. Where will you stay?
Surely not somewhere by yourself?"

His tone was sharp, and she started before silently remonstrating with herself. Perhaps she imagined the bite in his words?

"Mrs. Ellington said she knows of a young woman who will
accompany me to Spence's Hotel. I will stay there until I can find
more suitable lodgings."

The hatch opened, and bright light flooded the interior. She
cupped a hand above her brow and glanced at him. He frowned,
and she leaned out.

"You do not think that is appropriate?" she asked.

"Indeed, in the short term. Spence's at least will be comfortable, but if you would like, I can make enquiries to see what
lodging is available. You will want a house, I imagine?"

At her nod, he continued.

"That will mean staff. Once we arrive I will ask my own
people to investigate and find appropriate people."

"I do not wish to impose."

Relying on someone else wasn't something she was used to,
but now that she had taken the time to think about what he'd
said before, his offer made sense. She needed someone she could
lean on. Someone who could guide her in the short term and was
available to help her set up a household.

"It is no imposition at all."

He smiled, and she relaxed as he led her to the small seating
area the men had set up for the passengers of the *Zephyr*.

He waited while she sat before joining her. "I suppose it will
seem odd leaving the *Zephyr* after all this time?"

"Yes. We have been aboard for over four months. The journey
was long and quite tumultuous at the beginning. And I have a
hankering to be on dry land again."

Now that she was outside, just talking, the reality that they would soon be in a foreign land, surrounded by strangers, was overwhelming. Her sister was so ill, and the prospect of an extended stay in the infirmary crashed down on Elspeth. Her stomach jostled a little, like the flutter of a sail in the breeze.

Her lips trembled, and she hunted in her pocket for her handkerchief. "Oh dear!"

"Miss Forster, you are most unsettled." He leaned closer, and she turned away, unwilling for him to see the welling of tears.

"I'm... I'm well." The wobble of her voice was betraying, and he reached out, touching her arm lightly.

"Most people now make a full recovery from malaria. The infirmary really is the best place for her though. She will receive the very best care."

He spoke soothingly, and the tears ran faster, her stomach knotting. *Such an assurance is beyond his ability to deliver.* The thought made it seem more difficult to bear. *What if...*

"It isn't just that... I'll be alone. With no one I know. I've never..."

He slid his hand down to her wrist.

"In all my life, I've never really been alone. There have been friends. Family. Now... Once I leave this boat, I don't..." The words broke off on a sob.

"You won't be alone, Miss Forster." He reached up and swiped at her tears with gentle thumbs as she turned toward him.

Her consciousness told her he was too close, but the ache in her heart needed this embrace. Needed the touch. Anything that might soothe away the sudden and uncharacteristic panic that nearly overwhelmed her.

When he lowered his mouth to hers, it felt right. His lips were soft. He toyed and sipped, and an ache—warm and needy—grew inside her belly. She felt the touch of his tongue pressing at the seam of her lips.

Elspeth had been kissed before, but not with such all-consuming passion. They had been mere shadows of the emotions that surged deep within. She opened to him as his arms slid around her, enfolded her, and she gave up to the overwhelming pleasure that speared her center.

His mouth ranged over hers, the kiss deepened, making her body burn, while her hands ceased their fluttering to move up to his shoulders, which were broad and solid.

When he pulled away, she felt the loss. "I beg your pardon," he said.

Elspeth blinked. "What for?" The words escaped without thought, and he smiled before barking a laugh.

Then he pulled back and she remembered who he was, where they were, and the impropriety of their actions.

"Oh! Oh dear!" She blushed deeply, the red tide heating her skin as she turned away, resting her shaking hands on the railing. "You must think me excessively forward, Major." Her words sounded stilted to her ears, and he chuckled again before the sound died away.

"I think you are exceptionally alluring. But never forward." His voice was deep and brooding.

Unable to stop her reaction, she turned back to him. "No one has..." She stopped and bit her lip. She was being very fast.

"Then they are fools, if they cannot see the treasure before them." His harsh tone intrigued.

She wanted—needed—to know more and opened her mouth to seek clarification when she heard the call, "Miss Forster, can you come, please?"

The interruption broke the connection between them, and she stood and stepped away.

"If you'll excuse me?" Then she scurried across the deck toward Mrs. Ellington.

~

*T*hrough the dim, pre-morning light, he could see the city of Calcutta rising on the horizon. Here and there the masts of boats moored in the natural harbor moved with the light breeze.

Aeddan gripped the rails as he had every morning since boarding the vessel. Sleep had become a precious commodity, jarred by the increasingly frequent and highly erotic dreams he endured on a nightly basis, thanks to Miss Elspeth Forster.

"The woman has no clue." The small breeze stole his words.

"Major, no woman ever had a clue."

He smiled at Grundy's heartfelt comment. Army men, such as he, were staunch bachelors mostly. Entanglements of the marrying kind weren't for him yet, not until it was time to settle down and sell out of his commission. Then he'd take a wife and raise a family per tradition. Although, if he were honest with himself, this so-called tradition was little more than a screen that he, and many like him, hid behind.

Since meeting Miss Forster he'd wrestled with his conscience on more than one occasion about that.

She obviously wasn't a woman of loose morals. It was clear in the way she conducted herself. His own background caused him more than a few fraught moments. But now wasn't the time for dalliances, he firmly reminded himself.

She was interested and wanted to learn more about passion. The way she reacted was more than a simple indicator of that, even if she didn't realize it. God knew he was tempted to show her all—the ever-present erection in his trousers had become quite an embarrassment—but that would mean crossing a line. One he'd never before considered. She was gently born. A lady in all but name. For him to take advantage of her... That would be unconscionable.

"No, it would be worse than that," he muttered.

"Sir?" Grundy called out to him, but Aeddan simply shook his head.

"I will have to return home soon and take a wife. My father is aging."

There lay the truth. He had a responsibility to his family, to the line that stretched back generations. His wife must be well-bred and able to produce an heir. It was his responsibility to carry on the family name and safeguard the assets his forebears had amassed. *How I wish that fact to perdition.* Yet, Elspeth was all that and more.

Both he and Grundy knew his days of gallivanting were coming to an end. He'd promised Lytton one more mission. Then he would have to return to England, make his bow to his father, and do his duty. Never before had it felt like chains weighing him down, than at this moment.

The concept of the meek misses in white chilled him to his bones, and if he were to return home unwed, that was the future he had to look forward to. The thought of producing an heir with an insipid wife made him break out in a cold sweat.

"Major, you can't be serious? You'd give this excitement up for a woman?"

Aeddan bit back his reaction to Grundy's words. He hadn't ever wanted to. Not before. Somewhere, in the most deeply hidden recesses of his mind though, he thought that perhaps the fire and passion in Miss Elspeth Forster just might suit him. She was well-educated, thoughtful. Strong-willed. Beautiful. Accomplished.

She'd make an excellent wife for him. He gripped the side of the ship firmly, feeling the bite of wood in his palms.

He shied away, flicking the thought aside with a smooth movement of his hand. "Come, Grundy, I will have to marry soon. You know my situation."

Grundy frowned, his leathery countenance creasing further.

"If any of the hoity-toity misses from the upper-class circles 'ere are anything to go by, you'll be bored in a week."

He smiled. "Indeed, I probably would. But I'm not after just anyone." *No. Just anyone won't do for me.* The woman he married would have to be someone who could live with him in harmony. Someone with fire and passion.

The sound of footsteps had him turning. Miss Forster was making her way to the bow of the ship.

"Good morning, Major Fitzsimmons. Private Grundy." Her gown this morning was green and gold silk, fitting her like a glove, and for a moment, he wished he could touch her, just to remind himself of the warmth and suppleness of her skin.

She looked tired, and he wanted to hold out his hand and capture her in his arms. Calm the fears that upset her equilibrium. He itched to support her at a time when he knew she was stretched thin.

It was wholly unlike him.

"Captain Elliott assures me we should make landfall soon." She turned forward, as if determined to make the most of the situation.

"Your sister, she is better this morning?"

Her gloveless fingers, clutching the rail, became whiter. "No. She is a trifle worse. Mrs. Ellington shooed me out of the cabin for a spell while she prepares my sister. She assures me that by taking the air, I will increase my chances of avoiding the illness." The distraction in her voice spoke volumes.

"Once she is in the infirmary, the physicians will have her stabilized within days, I'm sure. Mrs. Ellington will stay with Miss Isabelle, won't she? Nurse her?"

"She will. Until Isabelle is recovered sufficiently, then we'll send her home." Her tone became remote, as if unsure of why he was enquiring.

"Good. Then Grundy will accompany your sister and Mrs. Ellington to the hospital, and I will accompany you to the hotel."

She stilled, her fingers releasing the rails. "Major, you are under no obligation to—"

"No, I am not. But I want to." He heard Grundy's attempt at covering a snort of laughter. He turned, casting a harsh eye on his man. "Grundy, go see if Mrs. Ellington requires anything and check with the captain as to the transportation of the luggage."

Grundy frowned before muttering under his breath and retreating.

"Thank you."

He turned back at her words and noted Elspeth surveying him.

She frowned. "I wanted to thank you properly, without an audience."

This time she instigated the touch of her lips, and he accepted it, slipping his arms around her body. Her mouth opened to him like a flower, and he plunged within. Tasting and sipping while she shyly returned the caress.

When her tongue touched his, he stiffened, his whole body tense. His head spun, and he wanted to pull back so he could ask her what she wanted. Damn it, he already knew what he would prefer, but throwing her to the deck was out of the question. The knowledge that the action was forbidden didn't make dealing with the intolerable ache of arousal any easier though.

When Elspeth pulled back Aeddan was nearly ready to throw her over his shoulder, but he locked the muscles of his legs and watched as she backed away. The small grin on her face faded as her eyes fluttered open.

"Oh dear. I do beg your pardon." She radiated the heat of a crimson blush.

"No. Don't apologize for the gift you have just accorded me."

She looked up, meeting his gaze. "But I..."

"You kissed me. And I enjoyed it. Never apologize for wanting to share such pleasure with me." A spark lit in her eyes, and

Aeddan slid his hand over her cheek. "If you were sure, and we had time, I would show you more."

Her eyes dilated at his words, and he knew the desire was shared on both sides. A roaring sense of triumph filled him.

"Once in Calcutta, I would like to..."

"Don't promise me something that you cannot deliver, Major Fitzsimmons. I don't cope with unfulfilled obligations at all well."

Her back straightened, and she stepped away, her face stony. With that, her face settled into a mask of resolution.

"Major? This must never happen again." This time her pale face was set before she whirled and left him.

The confusion at what had passed left him floundering. Wondering who had pledged exactly what, and how he'd gained an opportunity and squandered it.

# CHAPTER 5

$\mathcal{D}$ isembarking from the *Zephyr* was quicker than Elspeth had planned. She had met with the captain to make sure he had his orders and ensured that Isabelle was on her way to the infirmary. Then she refused to leave until all her baggage—and Isabelle's—was safely gathered onto a cart and the driver given explicit instructions for delivery. But the major had facilitated the acquisition of a carriage, joining her in the confined vehicle. It had parted the sea of people milling around. The squabs were deep, and she settled back as they left the noisy, crowded wharf.

Unable to resist, Elspeth pushed the curtains aside and took in the view. The sights were almost overwhelming. The exotic fabrics and fashions, cattle moving slowly down the roads. Her gaze darted to-and-fro as they rumbled through the sprawling city of Calcutta. Sounds intruded, the lowing of cattle, the yap of dogs, and the cries of men, women, and children. Soon they gave way to the hubbub of traffic whistles and cries as they moved into a more anglicized section of the city.

"So many cows. I can't believe they come and go at will," she said.

"Cattle are considered sacred here. No one interferes with them. There are also more structured levels of society. See those?" The major indicated people hanging back, their clothing faded and ill-fitting. Stains were evident on clothes, and children looked ragged. "They are the untouchables. The lowest of castes." The major reclined back in his seat.

"So much to learn. But I will." Elspeth contained the urge to crane through the window with excitement, while deep inside she wondered if she had bitten off more than she could handle. *What if this whole adventure goes wrong? What if Isabelle doesn't recover?* She tried to banish the thoughts, but they remained, gnawing at the edges of her mind.

A stinging pain caught her attention, and she realized she'd been chewing on her lip.

They'd come here on the pretext of learning more about their suppliers, but the added attraction of learning about passion had pushed her into agreeing.

Right now she felt lost in the general mass of the city.

Isabelle would be residing in the infirmary, and Elspeth had the most confusing feelings for Major Fitzsimmons. She acknowledged that she was attracted to him. But on his part she detected nothing more than the hope of a dalliance. *Would it be enough?*

His voice intruded on her thoughts. "If you look ahead, you will see the river from here."

She cast a glance in the direction he indicated. The brown river wound like a ribbon, following them on their travel.

Here and there buildings lined the streets. White monuments to the British régime, with large, arched windows marched in militaristic lines down the avenue. "The buildings are oddly decorated. They look English with the columns, yet the arches on the doors and windows..."

Major Fitzsimmons smiled. "That's the eastern influence. Did you not learn about that in the schoolroom?"

Elspeth blushed. "I was educated at home for the first few years, then sent to an academy where I learned the finer arts. When I returned home, I undertook to expand my knowledge of running the shipping lines. I had no time to investigate architecture and foreign lands."

"Forgive me. I just thought learning of the empire was part of the system of education."

She heard amusement color his tone and nearly gave in to the need to smile back.

Elspeth flicked an invisible piece of lint from her dress while she fought to control her reaction. Then she returned to studying the movements outside. Other carriages passed, and enquiring gazes met hers. The ladies either smiled or turned away in a haughty manner. *It's just like being at home.* She concealed the tiny laugh that rose with difficulty, her gloved fingers covering her lips. She didn't dare turn around to see if he, the major, was watching her.

The carriage pulled up outside an imposing stone building. A large Georgian square of white blocks, but gaily decorated with canopies of green. As the conveyance stopped under the portico, a doorman hurried to pull down the step and open the door for her. "Major! It's so good to see you again." The man scurried to help her from the conveyance while addressing Aeddan.

With great care, Elspeth stepped down onto the carpet and brushed her skirts to remove any wrinkles then straightened to her full height. Major Fitzsimmons took her arm, and together they made their way up the steps to the front door.

Once the wood and glass panels opened, they entered and she couldn't contain the gasp of amazement. "Why... It's breathtaking!"

"Yes. They do love their decoration here. Come, let us see you settled into your rooms, then I will leave you. I have business to attend to today."

Elspeth straightened up. "Major, thank you for your assistance today. I don't know how I would have managed."

He smiled for an instant, but it turned to a frown as she pulled away. "It was nothing."

Unwilling to impose on him further—after all, he'd just informed her he had other tasks to complete—she gifted him with an imperious nod of her head. "Good day, Major." Good manners would dictate that he'd accept her dismissal.

His frown deepened, but she softened the blow with a curtsey, and while his lips flattened she turned to face the liveried man.

"I am Miss Forster. You received a telegraph message?" She assumed her most haughty demeanor, and the man bowed. From the corner of her eye, she watched as the major made his departure, without another word, leaving her to deal with the obsequious man.

"Miss Forster, it is such an honor. And your sister?" He glanced around, no doubt surprised that a single woman would be traveling alone.

"She is in the infirmary, and will be joining me later. I will also have a young lady joining me as companion later today."

"Then let me show you to your rooms. I have arranged one with a balcony and private bathing room and sitting room for you, as per your request." He showed her up the stairs, which were wide and well-appointed.

They stopped on the second floor before large oak doors, inlaid with more gilt. Her breath caught as he pushed the doors open, revealing a large and carefully proportioned room of reds and golds. The chandelier sparkled in the sun, casting small droplets of reflected light here and there on the furniture. The chairs were plush and heavily carved, padded with rich brocades. The tables were highly polished wood, and everywhere was the scent of flowers.

"This is perfect," she said.

The man smiled. "And your stay? How long will we be graced with your company?"

"I don't know. Major Fitzsimmons suggested that he knew of a suitable house available, but I don't know how long that will take to arrange. And, of course, I am unsure how long my sister will be in the infirmary."

"Then you are welcome for as long as you wish to stay, Miss Forster." The man gestured to the corner of the room, where a long pull was suspended from the ceiling. "You will note there is a bellpull in each room, should you require service." With that he bowed himself out and she stood there, looking around.

She stepped to the window, removing her bonnet as she went. The large shutters pushed open at the touch of her hand, and she stepped onto the balcony, looking out over the city. It was so bright after the dimness of her suite that she needed to shade her eyes. Sounds, still so foreign to her, filled the air as she gazed at the vista before retreating within again.

The room had a number of doors leading off, so she entered the room to her left. It was a large, well-appointed bedroom, decorated with silk wallpaper in tones of gold and azure. She smiled. "Perfect. This will be my room." Off the room was a private bathing chamber and dressing room. "I wonder how long until my luggage arrives?"

She retreated out to the sitting room and through to the bedroom on the other side. This was shades of greens and golds. It too was luxurious with large cushions and a net curtain. The bathroom was just as finely laid out, with marble and gold fittings.

Two smaller rooms off the main room were servants' quarters, fitted out with a bed, mirror, washing facilities, drawers, and a chair. She was closing the door on one of the rooms when a knock sounded. After she opened the door, two burly men carried the trunks in and placed them where she directed, then she waited for them to leave.

Loneliness filled her as she stood in the empty rooms. "Perhaps a cup of tea." She headed for the bellpull and tugged. Tea worked wonders on any person's disposition.

~

*T*he missives arrived on Monday morning, as she dressed in the lightest summer gown she owned. "Jacinthe? My sister will be released from the infirmary tomorrow. I need to do something about searching for alternative accommodations."

The young girl, born of a native mother and an English soldier, nodded.

Mrs. Ellington had been right. Jacinthe was quiet but capable, schooled in many of the English ways and with a basic education. Exactly what Elspeth needed to navigate the ways of India. Not for the first time, she wondered if the girl would come with her, back to England, should she ask.

"Miss Elspeth, there is another."

Elspeth frowned, looking down at the silver salver. The handwriting was clearly masculine, written in a heavy script. For a moment her stomach quivered. Who could it be from? The only men she'd met so far were her agent and the major. She broke the seal as she sank into the chair.

> *Miss Forster,*
> *I have found suitable accommodation for you*
> *in a house to the north of Calcutta*
> *township. A carriage will collect you from*
> *your hotel tomorrow morning at ten o'clock*
> *and convey you there for an inspection. It*
> *has been empty for some time, but I believe*
> *it will serve your needs.*
> *AF*

Tomorrow morning? That meant she needed to prepare today. "Jacinthe?"

"Yes, Miss?" Jacinthe scurried into the room and hovered uncertainly.

"Is there some way you could find me willing helpers to prepare accommodation for my sister and myself, should we find the necessary accommodation? The major has informed me that he has found a house meeting my needs, but it's been empty for some time."

Jacinthe looked thoughtful. "I believe I know of those who would help clean. But what about staff, Miss?"

Now that the opportunity had presented itself, Elspeth was ready to leave the hotel. It had been both convenient and comfortable, but it would be better to set up house, allowing autonomy in her day-to-day movements.

"If the major is correct, then today we shall have to prepare the necessary items to move into the house, with your help, of course."

Jacinthe looked at the ground. "That I can, Miss, but…"

Elspeth smiled. "Well, you will come with me, won't you?"

Jacinthe stared at her, surprise clear for a moment before a broad grin split her berry brown face. "Yes, Miss."

Elspeth sipped at her tea, making a mental list of necessities she'd need for establishing a comfortable home. "Bring me my writing table as I need to send a message to my man of business. Then, I believe it's time we visited the markets."

Her task was accomplished quickly, and in no time, Jacinthe carried her bonnet over and Elspeth donned it, tying the strings firmly, followed by her lightest gloves. She reached for her bag.

"Do you have coin, Miss?"

Elspeth looked at her. "Coin?"

"To pay for the goods."

Elspeth stood stock-still. In England she had always placed

her purchases on account. She bit her lip. *So much to learn.* "Maybe we should go to the bank first."

The girl nodded and ushered her down the stairs. A carriage was called, and the next phase of her adventure began.

~

*E*lspeth entered the room, her skirts swishing over the cool tiles. The rooms were adequate, but dusty. It was obvious no female had inhabited this house for some time. The bedrooms would be comfortable, with large, net-covered tester beds. The coverlets and linen would need to be laundered though.

"How long did you say this house has been empty?"

The captain's wife, blousy and loud, hurried into the room, her steps echoing in the morning air. "Well, see, it's like this, Miss Forster. When the colonel's wife died in childbed he couldn't stay. He moved into the barracks."

Frustration filled her. She didn't need the history, just the length of time the house had stood empty. "Yes, yes. But how long?"

"Three years, Miss Forster."

"I will take it, but before I can lodge here with my sister, we will need a cleaning party. My maid..."

The large woman sniffed, and Elspeth sighed deeply. Her sister would be arriving from the infirmary tonight. There was a lot to do and not much time to achieve it in. More bodies would certainly make the task lighter to bear.

She cast a glance over her shoulder even as she stripped off her gloves. "I have goods arriving soon, and my maid will be bringing people in to help with the cleaning."

The woman left, muttering imprecations about mad newcomers from England. Elspeth didn't look in her direction, though the sound of retreating feet left her wondering what on earth she was doing.

She closed her eyes. She'd accepted this challenge and would see it through, whatever it brought. Inhaling deeply, she girded herself for the job ahead. "The bathing room first, I think."

She entered the room and cast a horrified glance at the hip bath. A layer of dust covered its surface. The detritus of who-knew-what bugs had settled, and she shivered at the horror before her. Isabelle would need a bath so best to get started, she reminded herself. But as Elspeth left the room to find the necessary equipment, she couldn't resist looking back at the bathing room.

After returning with a bucket and cloths, Elspeth stripped off the light coat, wishing she were back in the cool climes of England. She was thankful she'd worn an older gown for the inspection. She'd need to scrub the bath, and it wouldn't be a clean exercise.

She rubbed and rinsed as the temperature rose. "Dear me." The task was almost overwhelming, and she brushed a stray curl from her forehead. "Scrubbing this bath will probably take hours." She fretted, knowing all these jobs needed to be completed today.

*Knock.*

She half-rose, looking around. Lounging against the door-jamb was the gentleman she most wanted to avoid. *Major Fitzsimmons.*

"Miss Forster, I know I mentioned ladies falling at my feet, but surely this is excessive."

Her face flamed. He always seemed to catch her off-guard.

"Major, I can assure you, I have no intention of falling at your feet. No woman worth—"

"Miss Forster, I'm sure you protest too much." His words were languid.

He took a step toward her, moving slowly; the predator

seeking his prey. Her mouth dried, and her heart beat faster. She was the prey, and that knowledge left her feeling uncomfortable. Another emotion surged.

*Interest.* She refused to consider it. After all, she was no young miss... That reminder didn't help either.

"I'm waiting for assistance to arrive, Major."

He quirked his brow, and she nearly swallowed her tongue. If she wasn't a mature spinster, heaven help her, she'd probably swoon as she caught sight of the teasing glint in his eye. As it was, she struggled to hold onto her senses.

Elspeth turned back to the task before her. "I'll need fresh water, and more cleaning cloths..."

Warm, male hands settled on her shoulders. She shuddered at the feel of them. They exuded strength as he pulled her up. The grip was sure but cautious, as if he had no intention of dominating her.

"You need a man here to ensure your safety. Until we know who your servant has engaged, you shouldn't be left alone."

She stepped back, turning toward the wall, hoping to hide the confusion that filled her. Her stomach trembled. She was alone, with the major.

"Major, I am not a Miss out of the schoolroom. I can..." He stopped her words, swinging her around, his fingers digging into her shoulders.

"You don't know anything. You have no knowledge of the culture or the dangers. No idea what the men are capable of doing to a single, white female here. This is not London, and these are not civilized people." His voice was urgent and deep.

She twisted, trying to free herself from his grasp, but instead, he pulled her closer. Firmly against his chest.

"Listen to me!" His demand echoed.

Elspeth held herself still, her chest crushed against him. The sensations he aroused confused her, left her feeling weak, as if part of her had melted away. Heat built within her.

"Major, I—"

He swooped. His mouth descended on hers so fast she could only watch as his eyes darkened. Then their lips touched. Hers soft against his. They were harder than she expected. His mouth opened over hers, devouring while flames licked at the edges of her mind.

She opened her mouth and a sound rose in the quiet, little more than a mewl, but she ignored it. Pleasure speared her, rippling through her body. Crushed against him, she could hardly breathe. His scent filled her. He was intoxicating. The mixed aroma of horse, leather, and all man was overwhelmingly masculine.

Her body reacted as never before, and she continued on with the most outrageous actions. She slid her tongue along his as it entered her mouth. When his hand descended to her derriere though, firming over the swells, she stilled. Stiffened. Pulled away.

She knew her face was flaming. The heat scorched her skin. "How dare you, Major?"

His eyes glinted dangerously as he stepped back. Her body instantly felt the rejection. It cooled while her ire rose.

"Your behavior was..." At a loss for words, she watched as he smiled.

"Inappropriate? Yes, well. You make me want to do inappropriate things to you. With you." He leaned in closer. "I want to do them all night long." With a wink, he turned and strode away, stopping at the door for an instant. "I'll be here guarding you."

Then he left the room.

~

*H*er face was still flaming as she scrubbed the tub viciously. "Jacinthe, I'll need more water."

Another girl hurried to obey, the edges of her saree flapping around her legs as she carried the bucket of clean water.

"The major... He wants to know how long you will be, *memsahib*?"

Elspeth shook her head. "I don't know. Tell him I will be occupied for some time, and hope to be moving in later today."

Jacinthe disappeared, shushing the other girl as she went, before returning. "The major says he will wait."

Elspeth closed her eyes for an instant, but knew he wouldn't leave until she had faced him.

"And where do you want the boxes of items that have arrived?" Jacinthe asked.

Elspeth stood, pushing back strands of hair from her sweat-slicked face. "What goods?"

"The kitchen items have arrived, along with the new linen. The trunks have just been delivered from the hotel, and I have instructed the cook to find the foodstuffs you requested."

"The kitchen items in the kitchen, my trunks in the largest room, and my sister's in the smaller. The linen in the laundry if it's ready." She spoke absently as she regarded herself in the mirror.

"Yes, *memsahib*."

"Then find me a clean towel, some water, and a brush." She would make herself presentable before facing the major.

The girl scurried off, and Elspeth removed the old sheet she had tied around her waist during her cleaning spree. Jacinthe returned and Elspeth accepted the items from her, then she cleaned herself up, tidied her hair, and washed her hands and face.

"I will finish in here, unless you wish something else?"

Elspeth spared a glance at the young woman. "Actually, I think some tea would be welcome. Is the verandah clean enough to use?"

The girl bobbed her head in agreement, and Elspeth stepped out of the bathing room.

The hustle and bustle of people was making short work of cleaning the house. The floors were immaculate already, large rugs were being replaced after a good beating, and the dust on the furniture had been swept away. She found herself running her fingers along the now cleansed furnishings.

On the verandah the major waited, hip against the wooden doorjamb and a broad smile on his deeply tanned face. The wicker furniture had been brushed and wiped until it gleamed in the sunlight.

"Your army has worked wonders on this house. You should be very comfortable here."

"Indeed, Major. My sister and I foresee staying for at least several months, so it makes sense to be comfortable. Now I have ordered tea. You will take some with me, won't you?"

He frowned, as if he hadn't expected her to invite him to join her, then bowed. "It would be my pleasure."

She might feel hot and more than slightly grubby, but social niceties had been ingrained first by her mother and then by the ladies who ran the small school she had attended.

He waited until she sank onto the small chair, then took a seat himself. They made small talk as they waited for the tea to be delivered.

Elspeth poured and handed a cup to her guest. They continued discussing the weather, the state of the markets in downtown Calcutta, and even her home as they drank, always circling around the awareness that drew her eyes back to his time and again.

The fan above her head moved slowly back and forth as the punkhawallah attended to his job of keeping the air circulating. Finally, Major Fitzsimmons rose. "Thank you for your hospitality. I should leave now but will return tomorrow, unless you require—"

"Nonsense, there is no need for you to remain here. Jacinthe is here with me, and Isabelle will be arriving soon. Jacinthe has organized for a man to also be here, I believe he is her uncle and he is recommended to me. We will be quite secure, I assure you."

His face tightened with disapproval.

"Besides, we are within the limits of town. There are houses either side of us. Why Colonel Montague lives next door and Sir Peter Caravel on the other side. We will hardly be alone and unprotected."

"Indeed, then I will take my leave, Miss Forster." He smiled, his eyes twinkling with some kind of devilry that she couldn't decipher.

Elspeth rose and held out her hand, expecting nothing more than a casual touch of fingers in the socially accepted manner. He held her hand, his clasp firm. She gave a tiny squeeze then released him. Instead of reciprocating, he ran his thumb up her palm, over the mound, and to the sensitive skin at the base of her wrist, while his gaze captured her. Held her in thrall. Then, with a light movement, he grazed his thumb over her skin.

She couldn't contain the sigh that escaped her lips.

"And I will bid you adieu, Miss Forster."

She waited for him to release her, her breath caught in her throat.

"Elspeth." Then, with a wink, he let go and left her, bewildered and alone.

# CHAPTER 6

*A*eddan walked through the crowded streets, thinking over the last time he'd seen the woman whom bedeviled him with the storm of emotions he'd seen hidden in the depths of her gaze. The heat in her responses, especially when they escaped her iron-clad restraints. Perhaps he was being foolish, but remonstrating with himself made no difference. The incident in the bathing room had reinforced just how attractive he found her.

In vain, he'd sought to banish the memories, concentrating on his task and the demands of Lord Lytton. In the days since last seeing Elspeth, he'd felt on edge. *Raw.* He hated feeling out of control.

The heat of the morning sun beat down on him as he entered the building and walked down the cool corridor of power. The squeak of feet on the tiles echoed. This was something he understood, could deal with. He breathed deeply, settling his mind on his set task as he rounded a corner to see his destination waiting just ahead.

"Major Fitzsimmons?" Lytton's secretary's words broke through his thoughts.

"Yes. I'm here to see Lord Lytton."

The man was short and wiry, his glasses perched on the end of his nose, but he carried an air of self-possession about him. "If you will take a seat, Major, I will see if his lordship will attend you." He gave a snappy nod, turned on highly polished, squeaking shoes, and sauntered off.

Aeddan suppressed the desire to ignore the annoyingly officious man and march into the room, but instead settled himself on the uncomfortable timber chair. He'd only been there a matter of minutes when the heavy wood door opened and Lord Lytton stepped toward him.

Lytton had an aristocratic high forehead and sleepy eyes that belayed the keen intelligence of the man. He also carried an air of command. "Come in, Fitzsimmons."

Aeddan stood, brushed down his pant leg, and entered the room after his lordship. "Sir."

"So, what did you learn? We've been waiting for you to return with the information. You made excellent time."

Aeddan handed him the packet of papers, which Lytton accepted and opened.

He scanned the documents, then laid them on his table. "Your thoughts?"

Aeddan ran through the mass of impressions he had collected during his time in Kabul. "It would seem the Russian contingent is hopeful of forming an alliance with the Sheh, but he's dismissed their request, for now. However, there is chatter in the markets that there are still pockets of resistance since the ousting of Mohammad Afzal Khan."

"Hmm." Lytton frowned, rubbing is beard as he walked around the imposing desk filling the middle of the room. "And you think this might—"

"If anything, I think he may be more inclined to remain neutral. He's taken that stand since regaining his position as Amir in sixty-eight."

Lytton stopped, his back to Aeddan, and not for the first time, Fitzsimmons wondered at the machinations that brought a man like this to India.

The room was silent but for the occasional tick of the clock in the corner.

"I know you wish to be released from your duties to the crown, but I have one more role for you to play. Over the next several months, I need someone to keep their ear to the ground here in Calcutta and to take a journey into the interior. Listen to the ordinary people and gain their perspective. I believe there are those who would undermine our position here."

"But sir..." He lurched, gritting his teeth. He had responsibilities and a future to plan.

Lytton looked at him, his face hard and his gaze as flat as any warrior's. "I need men I can trust. I have sent another envoy to Kabul, demanding the opportunity for a mission. I believe it will fail, and we will possibly need to force the issue. I need someone here, in southern India, to investigate the rumors of a leak. I need someone the crown can trust."

Aeddan tensed. "I need to return home. My father—"

"Yes, he's aging. But if we can't fortify the empire, then you may have less of a title to return to. I need your help, man. We have many fronts on which the empire remains in jeopardy. Your empire needs help. Your queen needs your skills."

Aeddan ground his teeth together. He was no one's fool, because if what Lytton was asking for was indeed as important as he said, then truly everything they had achieved so far was in danger. Lytton wouldn't make such a request lightly.

"And then..."

"Then you will be free to travel home and take up your position in society."

Even as Lytton spoke, the familiar heaviness of his future crashed down upon him. A wife. Children. Would they be able to fulfill him as effectively as his work for the crown?

"Now, I hear Forster Shipping arrived with some extra cargo? My wife is most keen to meet Miss Forster and her sister. I believe you have been offering her some assistance?" The lightning change in conversation momentarily took Aeddan by surprise.

"Err, yes. Miss Forster has taken up residence in a vacant house with her sister." He was uncomfortably aware that Lytton was sizing up his reaction to the change of conversational tack. "She wishes to learn more about her suppliers."

Lytton lowered himself into his leather chair. "Take a seat, Aeddan, because I think this might be the opportunity we are looking for."

~

"Isabelle, do you feel up to socializing, dearest?" Elspeth picked the invitation up from the table. Over the last week, the pile had grown daily. "We really should make an effort, if you feel improved." She turned, her gown swishing a little on the tiled floor.

"Oh, sister, I feel so much better. Yes, I believe it is time for us to enter society. Do you think Major Fitzsimmons will be attending?"

The major had called several times to check everything was as it should be. It left her wondering on more than one occasion just what dark game he was engaged in.

"I believe he will, Isabelle. But oh dear, whatever will we wear? Most of our gowns are heavy and with this heat..."

Jacinthe entered the room, the padding of her soft slippers barely making a sound. "I know of a dressmaker. She's quick and does quality work. And what's more, many of the *memsahib*'s wear pale colors, so you could choose paler tones, which are cooler." She moved around the room, collecting their hats and parasols. "If you wish, she can come here to do your fittings. And her fees are very reasonable too."

Elspeth had already discovered just how reasonable most vendors were in India. She made a split-second decision. "Yes, send for her. How soon might she have a gown ready for us, do you think?"

"It may take her a day or two, depending on how many others she can find to work on the gowns at the same time." Jacinthe bowed deeply, as was her way.

Elspeth smiled. Certainly this would be an easy way of upgrading their wardrobe quickly and inexpensively, and perhaps the woman would be willing to discuss her sources of materials. "Excellent then. Now, let us check through the invitations at hand, so we can plan."

Jacinthe bowed once more and left Elspeth alone with Isabelle.

"Elspeth, Jacinthe is a treasure. And her voice? It lilts so beautifully. I wonder... Do you think she would come back to England with us when we leave here? I've become quite fond of her in these last couple of days. And without Ellie..." Isabelle's voice trailed away.

"I do hope so. She has already become quite invaluable to me. She's skilled with hair and mending, and she is also excellent company." Elspeth lowered herself carefully into the well-padded seat as the door opened once more.

Isabelle straightened up as Jacinthe entered the room. "I'm sorry to intrude, but Major Fitzsimmons is at the door."

"Do show him in, Jacinthe."

The girl bobbed a curtsy and disappeared only to return with the major at her heels. Elspeth rose, uncertain what he might want with her today.

"Ladies. I do hope I haven't caught you at an inopportune time? Miss Isabelle, I'm pleased to see you are improving in health. Why, you look positively lovely."

Isabelle glowed under his enthusiastic greeting, and an

uncomfortable emotion filled Elspeth. Taking her seat, Elspeth waited for him to settle opposite her.

"I came to see if you'd be interested in attending a small soirée. Lady Lytton is hopeful that you would and sent me to enquire about the possibility."

Elspeth watched him, just as she had every other time he'd called. He was comfortable in the social setting, expansive even. He smiled easily and wore civilian clothes as if they were his usual garb.

"We were just planning on discussing the invitations at hand. Let me see..." She flicked through those in her grasp, spying the one of which he spoke, the dark script outlining the details. "Oh yes. Tomorrow? Well, I'm sure we could attend, as long as Isabelle feels up to it."

Isabelle smiled broadly. "Oh, that would indeed be a grand outing. I'm rather looking forward to seeing something other than here."

"That's settled then. I'll bring my carriage."

Isabelle beamed while the tea trolley rumbled into the room. Elspeth concentrated on pouring the drinks as Major Fitzsimmons chatted with Isabelle. She gritted her teeth, fending off the horrible emotions that roiled deep within her belly.

"Major?"

He accepted the cup and gazed at her with a probing glance, leaving her with the uncanny feeling that he could read her emotions.

Isabelle took hers and sipped cautiously, the room almost silent except for the clatter of spoons and the sipping of tea.

Now the silence stretched out. Elspeth had no wish for making small talk, Isabelle had obviously worked out there was some kind of...*air* between them, and the major kept shooting her looks of amusement. *It really is quite vexing!*

Once the teas were drunk, he rose. "If you would excuse me, Miss Isabelle, I'd like to talk to your sister for a moment."

Isabelle's face blanked carefully, but Elspeth could read the surprise in her eyes. "Of course, Major. If you'll excuse me?"

She rose then left the room, leaving Elspeth quite uncomfortably aware of the impropriety of their actions.

"Major? What could you wish to raise with me?"

He settled back into the seat he'd vacated. "I'm very concerned that you plan to visit your suppliers without adequate protection. I have spoken with Lord Lytton, and he has kindly arranged for an escort, including myself and Grundy, to travel with you. He feels it is better that a lady such as yourself have suitable protection."

Elspeth was unsure what to say to his kind words. "I'm overwhelmed, Major. Though thankful for his lordship's concessions, might I think on it? I have specific locales I wish to see."

"Of course."

This time when he rose she moved toward him, stretching out her hand. He took it, and the sensation of heat she now associated with him filled her. "I appreciate everything you have done for us."

His smile died away, replaced with what she could only call hunger. "Not for everyone... For you...*Elspeth*."

Without another word he bowed and turned, leaving her to watch the door shut behind him.

~

*E*lspeth trembled like a leaf in the wind, even though she fought to control her body's reaction. Major Fitzsimmons was due any moment. Isabelle waited with her in the parlor; her gown of peacock blue emphasized her pale beauty, her sparkling eyes, and silvery blonde hair. Beside her, Elspeth felt like a sparrow—dark and drab.

Her gown of burnished copper fit like a glove, although maybe a little too snugly around her bosom, and with her hair caught up high, it emphasized her height. She was taller than most of her counterparts, which meant she was forever towering over them. Not a positive first sign with prospective suitors, she thought sourly.

Elspeth raised her arm, patting her hair again with her hand. "Are you sure this looks...appropriate?"

Isabelle smiled. "Of course. Now do sit down! It is making me dizzy watching you pat and preen."

Those words stopped her in her tracks. *Am I?* Did she really care what Major Fitzsimmons thought of her? Then she laughed silently. Of course she did. She had been like that since she'd met him aboard the *Zephyr*.

The door opened behind her. "Major Fitzsimmons." Jacinthe's voice echoed in the now quiet room.

Elspeth sucked in a deep breath and pasted on a smile, fighting the butterflies that took wing inside her stomach.

He entered the room, looking dashing in his formal uniform of a dark blue single-breasted tunic featuring ten highly polished, brass buttons and decorated with red piping. His black boots shone in the light of the lamps, and for a moment her breath fled.

As she regained her composure his gaze roamed over her and she fancied that she saw approval in his eyes. "Miss Forster, you look quite lovely."

The touch of his hand on hers warmed her. Then he turned toward her sister, and the warmth which had spread through her at his gaze dissipated.

"Miss Isabelle, what a delightful ensemble." He bowed over Isabelle's hand, but Elspeth fancied he didn't hold it for quite as long as hers.

*Elspeth, you're being quite fanciful!*

He proffered his arm to Elspeth as the older sister, and she took it, grateful for her long gloves, otherwise she was sure that the shock of connection would scorch her. They proceeded down the hall to the front door, which Jacinthe held open, and he handed them into the carriage.

Behind her, Isabelle chattered gaily.

The ride to the Vice Regal house was short. They swept through the gates and up a long and imposing drive, but waiting to alight their carriage took a considerable period of time. Elspeth remained in her seat, pretending to look out the window as the horses clattered on cobblestones. The streets had emptied, and the sun sat low on the horizon.

She listened idly as Isabelle and the major chattered. "Who will be there?" It was unlike Isabelle, but since her illness, she seemed to have discovered her social skills. Elspeth didn't mind, however, as her sister was whole and well.

Elspeth used the wait to center herself. Such outings had been out of her realm of experience at home, with the clearly defined social status being rigidly observed. She fiddled with her gown, straightened her skirt, toyed with the light wrap she'd slipped around her shoulders, and wondered what the ladies here would make of her.

Major Fitzsimmons leaned slightly in her direction, and his voice cut through the silence. "You look breathtaking."

"I... Uh..." Elspeth drew in an unsteady breath. "Thank you, Major."

"Aeddan."

"Pardon?" She gave him what she supposed was a startled look.

He smiled, white teeth flashing in the gloom. "My name is Aeddan."

*Aeddan.* The name suited him. It was strong. Assured.

They drove up to the door, then the major stepped down, and Isabelle alighted. As Elspeth made to exit the carriage, Aeddan held her hand for just a moment longer than usual before letting it go with a searching look. In that short time, her breath caught in her throat.

She glanced away, unable to find her equilibrium, and bit her lip, before pinching her cheeks to brighten them slightly.

Aeddan propelled her forward, and she stumbled a little, but he was there, lending her support. Up the white stairs they moved. Then Isabelle and Elspeth's wraps were whisked away, before they moved into the room where everyone gathered.

The room was full, with glittering lights and music, chatter and satins and silks. Once again Elspeth felt gauche and uneducated as she stared at the throngs before her. The fans moved lazily overhead. The major surged forward, comfortable in the environment, and not for the first time, Elspeth wondered about this man. He was an enigma, clearly as at home here in the gay and moneyed atmosphere as he was striding through the dusty streets or aboard a ship.

"Let me introduce you."

He stopped before one unmistakably beautiful woman with a fine gown. Her hair was piled in an elegant knot atop her head, although, quite scandalously, there was a detectable thickness at the waist of her gown. Elspeth knew that meant she was *enceinte*.

"Ma'am, allow me to introduce Miss Forster and her sister, Miss Isabelle Forster."

Both Isabelle and Elspeth dropped a curtsey to the woman, and she inclined her head. There was something regal about her that prompted their actions.

"So this is Miss Forster? Come walk with me a while, dear."

Aeddan bowed low, but there was a frown on his face as he backed away.

*Who is this woman, and what does she want with me?* Elspeth decided the best course of action was to wait.

"La! I suppose I didn't even give Aeddan time to introduce me. I am Lady Lytton. Now, I understand you and your sister run your family shipping business. I find that utterly fascinating. I myself am in favor of women being educated and holding useful positions in society, but opportunities are rare."

"Indeed, ma'am? I'm greatly encouraged to hear that at least some women see the value in education and vocation."

"Yes, Miss Forster. I rather think you would enjoy that given your own position with Forster Shipping." When Elspeth craned her neck in the woman's direction, Lady Lytton laughed and tapped her on the arm with her fan. "I've asked around about you. I appreciate a woman who knows her mind. Come and visit me one day for afternoon tea. I would be greatly interested in your thoughts." Thus dismissed, Lady Lytton wandered off, to be caught up in groups of gaiety.

"Well, it seems you made your mark."

Elspeth jumped, hearing Aeddan's voice behind her. She hadn't heard him approach.

"Major Fitzsimmons! You startled me." She raised a hand to her chest, covering her now rapidly beating chest.

His eyes turned grave. "Then I do beg your pardon, Miss Forster. Allow me to introduce you around?"

She nodded before turning to look for her sister. "Isabelle?"

"Is already ensconced among a group of ladies. I believe they wish to know more about her gown." His voice was determinedly bland.

"Then by all means, lead on, kind sir."

The evening passed in a whirl of social niceties, though Elspeth had the distinct impression she was being sized up by many of the ladies attending, particularly those of the unmarried variety. Aeddan remained attentive throughout the soirée, rarely leaving her side. She was aware of him, the heat that radiated from him, and the zing she experienced in his company.

Finally, the evening drew to a close and they headed back to the house she and her sister were renting.

Jacinthe had waited up and opened the door. Isabelle, clearly exhausted, bade them goodnight then left them alone in the parlor.

"Major..."

"*Aeddan.* Say it. *Aeddan.*" His words were like a drug, and she gave in.

"Aeddan..." Her stomach knotted. "I... Would you like a drink of something?" A sense of desperation filled her. *Here is a man who could teach me of pleasure, but would he? Or will he fall back on his scruples and deny me the experience?* Perhaps she radiated some hint of her thoughts, because he frowned.

"No. Not tonight. Tomorrow is the Rollington's Ball. You will attend?"

He gazed at her, eyes lazy yet holding an awareness that sent shivers down her spine. She was fascinated at the play of emotions in his eyes.

"We intend to be there."

He smiled, and her breath caught once more.

"Excellent. Now I will bid you goodnight, Elspeth." He stepped forward, slid his arms around her waist, and tugged.

She fell against him as his lips touched hers. The kiss redolent with sizzling intensity. The wild conflagration grew between them, burning hot. He devoured with lips and tongue. Drawing her deeper into the web he wove... Sensual. Erotic. His arms held her close so that every inch of their bodies touched. Even through the layers of fabric a zing arced between them.

Hunger filled her, warming the pit of her belly, and she tingled. All over. Hints of forbidden pleasure warmed and swelled.

When Aeddan pulled away, she panted and heat scorched her skin. "Aeddan..." She couldn't help the question that rose.

"Not tonight. Soon." Then, with a bow, he turned and left her standing there, watching his unhurried retreat.

# CHAPTER 7

*G*rundy popped his head around the door. "Major? There's a boy, come with a message from his lordship."

Aeddan had been looking at the same reports for an hour, calculating the information contained within them. Gathering the intelligence that would let him prove that there was a mole within the government ranks.

"Who is it?"

"Don't know 'im, Major. Reckon he's new." Grundy obviously wasn't sure though; it was clear in the doubtful tone of his voice.

"Right. I'll come out then." He rose, pushing back from the table and stretching. He hadn't yet found anything untoward in the notes he'd been reading. Perhaps this was what he needed?

A young boy, probably around ten, waited in the cool foyer, his white kurtah impeccably clean. "*Sahib*? I bring a note from Lord Lytton. He says to hand it to you alone." He spoke with the rapid-fire lilt Aeddan had grown used to in India.

He took the note, broke the seal, and scanned it.

*It would seem that Miss Forster has taken the
eye of the mole. They have arranged for an*

> *escort, including Major Albemarle and*
> *Colonel Fortescue and their men, to*
> *accompany her. You will need to move*
> *quickly to offset this. RBL*

"Albermarle and Fortescue." He muttered to himself, but Grundy's eyes narrowed at his words.

"What? Major?"

"We must go out. Prepare a carriage immediately." He turned back to the boy. "Come with me."

Quick strides saw him in his office, and he opened the drawer of his desk, reached for a piece of parchment and his pen. Sure strokes marked the paper as he scratched out his response.

> *I will attend Miss Forster immediately and*
> *ensure that she does not accept their offer of*
> *escort. Will report later. AF*

"Give this to his lordship. No one else," he instructed.

He didn't know why Albemarle and Fortescue might be focusing on Miss Forster, but the primal urge to protect her had risen. The emotion was unfamiliar, yet not *unsettling.*

He had no time to ponder it as the boy hurried out the door, berry brown fingers curled around the shilling Aeddan had given him. As soon as the boy was gone he strode out of his office, taking the steps to the sleeping areas two at a time.

Once within his room he headed for the wardrobe and snatched up his coat, uncaring of the items that were knocked from the stand. He shrugged into it and headed back downstairs and out the door.

Grundy was just pulling the carriage around as he exited the house. "Good thing you were planning on going out soon, Major. Siraj was already preparing the carriage and horses."

"Good. You're with me, Grundy."

His man looked a little surprised, but nodded and took up the reins. "Very good, Major."

Aeddan climbed in. "We need to see Miss Forster."

Grundy cast him a surprised glance but wisely kept his own counsel as they made their way down the drive. The traffic on the roads was bustling. Carts and cattle swarmed while people wandered backward and forward in front of the carriages.

Slowly, they moved forward, heading in the direction of the north end of the town. His fingers tapped out a wild tattoo until in the distance he spied the façade of Miss Forster and her sister's house. In front stood two carriages. One belonged to Lady Manton. The other he knew well too, and he swore. Fortescue was already here.

The conveyance came to a halt, and Aeddan sprang to the ground. "Wait for me."

He could feel the weight of Grundy's gaze as he made his way to the front door. It opened at his knock. Young Jacinthe smiled at him as she allowed him entrance before closing the door on the heated afternoon sun.

"Come this way, Major."

He followed her to the small sitting room, where Lady Manton, in her most elegant day gown, sat on the chaise lounge with Miss Isabelle. Miss Forster—Elspeth—captured his attention, looking ravishing in a pale green dress that picked up the tones of her eyes.

"Major Fitzsimmons, Miss Forster."

He bowed low at Jacinthe's words and entered the room, taking in the tableau in an encompassing glance. Fortescue and Albemarle stood off to the side, as Elspeth was serving tea.

"Why, Major! It's so good to see you today." Elspeth's eyes flashed as she smiled her welcome to him alone. She lowered the china pot to the tiny table before her. "Jacinthe? I'll have a cup for the major, please."

The young girl hurried out of the room and Aeddan bowed to

her ladyship, who smiled and inclined her head regally in his direction.

"Major, it is good to see you again." Isabelle glowed quietly before Lady Manton engaged her in conversation once more.

He narrowed his gaze on Albemarle and Fortescue who accepted their tea and moved back against the wall, talking quietly among themselves.

"Miss Forster, I have come to enquire if you would be willing to allow me to escort you to the silk markets later this week?"

She smiled at him. "I would very much enjoy that."

He noted from the corner of his eye as Fortescue frowned. He'd need to push carefully now, so it didn't tip his hand.

"Of course, I'm also aware that you wished to visit the areas of silk production. I had thought perhaps Baharampur? It would take some time, but..." He waited a beat as the two men straightened.

"Excuse me, Major. That's not the done thing! How will you arrange for a chaperone for Miss Forster when you're a single man?" Fortescue's spirited defense made him want to smile.

"Oh, that's already taken care of. Well, Miss Forster? Will you join me?"

She looked at him, no doubt questioning his sanity after his arguments with her aboard the *Zephyr*.

"Indeed, sir. I would certainly appreciate your escort." She looked as if she had more to say, but Lady Manton indicated her wish to leave by rising. Elspeth and Isabelle and himself followed suit as was expected in polite company.

"Now I must leave you, my dear. Think on what I have spoken to you about today. Miss Isabelle, I am pleased you are recovered. Fortescue and Albemarle, I believe you have a parade soon? You may escort me out." As Lady Manton passed by Aeddan, she placed her hand on his shoulder and whispered, "Take great care of her. The sharks have already begun circling."

Then the woman bustled from the room, followed by the two

men Aeddan knew were unhappy at the turn of events they couldn't control.

Elspeth took her seat again as the door shut with a near silent click. "Well then. What day would be suitable to you?" She turned toward him, and the smile on her face stole his breath. Her eyes twinkled, and the pink of her cheeks was more than just becoming.

Jacinthe cracked open the doors. "Excuse me, Miss Forster, but could Miss Isabelle join me? The seamstress is here."

Aeddan made to rise, but Isabelle stood and granted him a sweet grin.

"No, you stay, Major. I have some gowns that required extra fittings." With a nod she was through the door.

"I'm going to be busy for the next few days, however, I have no further commitments after Thursday next. Does that suit you?" he asked Elspeth. "As to the other visit to Baharumpur, I will arrange for a chaperone for you. Also the guards that will be necessary for our safety."

"Yes, that suits me well. I need to make arrangements for things while I'm gone. Then there is the packing of clothing and making arrangements for Isabelle. You will let me know when you're ready?"

Elspeth was unlike any other woman of his experience. No one could call her a ditherer.

"Indeed I shall. Excellent." He stood. He should leave, but he suddenly hungered to stay longer.

Elspeth watched him, worrying her full lower lip with her teeth. "Aeddan, I..." She blushed a deep red.

He frowned, wondering what concerned her now. She rose, her hands now fluttering like tiny butterflies, and she straightened the skirt of her gown.

"What's wrong, Elspeth?"

She glanced in his direction, and he saw the hunger in her

eyes. The innocent fire he recognized in her gaze teased his senses. Without conscious thought, he closed the distance between them. Aeddan was almost there when his mind questioned his action, and he stopped.

Now he watched her. Waited, his heart thudding in his chest wildly. What would she do?

She smiled shyly and took the last step, right up to him. He opened his arms, and she slid her fingers around his waist.

He bent his head, inhaling the subtle scent of roses, watching her eyes darken, until his lips met hers. Mouths ground against each other as the hunger exploded deep in his belly. He grasped her waist, tugging her more firmly against him, and he felt hesitant, shy fingers curl into his hair.

She tasted sweet. Hot and intoxicating. He gloried in the sensations, the scents, and the taste. She mewled in her throat, and he wanted to roar his triumph. She was his, surely?

Behind him came a sound, tugging him from the cloud of arousal he'd given into. "Uh, excuse me..."

*Jacinthe. Damn!* Would there never be time or privacy with this woman?

Elspeth pulled away from his embrace, panic and embarrassment leaving pink streaks over her cheeks, her eyes wide, and the look was like a punch in the gut. She turned away, her skirts swirling, as her hands moved over her hair.

"Jacinthe?"

"Uh, Miss Isabelle asked me to let you know the seamstress is ready for you."

Elspeth turned back. Her eyes still glittered with the final vestiges of excitement, but the pink was fading.

*Time to leave. For now anyway.*

He straightened. "I will bid you good day then, Miss Forster."

He bowed deeply, watching her, telling her with his eyes that they would continue this exploration of the senses. He knew the second she understood. It was clear in the way her eyes widened. Then her face settled into a serene smile.

"Good day, Major."

With that, he turned and left the room.

# CHAPTER 8

*E*lspeth's stomach quivered. She had tried and discarded four gowns before finally settling on the bronzed silk. It was almost severe in cut, the only adornment a decorative sweep of tiny pearls sewed to the bodice.

Tonight she felt different, as if there was some momentous event about to take place. She gripped her fan of ivory and silk and tugged the wrap more firmly around her. Aeddan's note had instructed that they wait for him.

The scent of jasmine filled the air, and she wandered to the window, chancing a look outdoors.

"He'll be here soon enough, my love. Will you not sit down beside me? I feel positively slothful watching you pace back and forth." Isabelle's voice rang like a bell, and Elspeth turned to look at her.

"I..." How could she explain to Isabelle that she was about to take a leap into the unknown? To follow through on the daring plan they'd hatched months ago in the drawing room? "Aeddan... He's..."

Isabelle's eyes widened. "Has he... Has he asked you?" Her voice was little more than a squeak, and Elspeth cringed.

"Not in so many words." She turned back as the sound of hooves and wheels on cobbles filled the air. "He's here." Elspeth remained looking out, ending any further discussion with her sister on the subject.

Aeddan entered the room. His dark attire accentuated the breadth of his shoulders. He bowed to both of them. "Ladies. You both look quite ravishing."

Elspeth accepted his proffered arm.

"If you're ready then?"

Isabelle rose and looked at her with an I-want-to-know-more-later look and preceded them to the hallway.

Elspeth made to move, but for an instant, Aeddan held her back. His gaze was smoldering. "Your sister is ravishing, but you are breathtaking, Elspeth."

The words left her a shivering mass of nerves.

Aeddan led her to the door and assisted her into the carriage, his hand resting just longer than propriety allowed on the curve of her waist. Elspeth didn't know if Isabelle had noticed that or not.

The ride was quick, and as they arrived strains of music echoed. If not for the humidity, she was sure she could have been back in England.

On Aeddan's arm she entered the ballroom. Men in a mixture of uniforms and black suits paraded and danced with women dressed in an array of finery. The crystal chandeliers sparkled as laughter, chatter, and music filled the air.

Aeddan dipped his head to hers. "Grant me your first dance," he said, then introduced her to his friends.

Isabelle had already found a group of young women who engaged her in conversation, and she waved them on with a searching look at Elspeth.

A waltz struck up, and Aeddan excused them from their current set of acquaintances with a, "My dance, I believe."

"Major, should we be dancing this? I'm not sure..."

His arms already encircled her, pulling her into the seething mass of bodies. As they came together on the dancefloor a shiver betrayed her inner turmoil.

"There is nothing fast in waltzing. It is now widely accepted, even in London."

Elspeth gave a small nod to show her understanding while her body trembled with the desire she'd been fighting since their first meeting. She was so close to him she could feel the warmth and strength of his body. He guided her smoothly across the polished floor with skill and agility. He didn't speak, but the touch of his fingers caressed her bared skin at her wrist, above the silk of her glove that had slid down.

As the music drew to a close she chanced to look at him. His eyes were slumberous.

"Come with me," he requested quietly.

There was an unspoken invitation to passion that she now understood. He wanted her as much as she wanted him.

Elspeth took a shallow, unsteady breath and nodded. She would go with him. Accept the licking flames of passion she spied burning in his careful gaze. But even as she took his arm she was aware that her sister was watching.

They walked slowly out of the room, onto the terrace, heavily scented with jasmine and honeysuckle, the sounds of the ball behind them. She was sure they'd stop there, but he urged her further to the end of the veranda and to a dimly lit hallway.

"Where are we going?" She could barely speak, and swallowed.

"The library," he said. "I acquired the key earlier today from the colonel."

She looked away. He'd planned it all. Was it the right thing to do? She was both exhilarated and frightened at the step she was taking. She followed him through the open veranda door, deep carpeting muffling the sound of their footsteps.

Together they walked down the corridor, past closed doors.

He stopped her. "If we take this step, there can be no turning back, Elspeth. I want you. You want me. Yes?"

Her stomach quivered. *Last chance, Elspeth,* she told herself. "I do."

"Then will you let me show you a world of pleasure?" Even in the half-light, she detected need on his face. The way it tightened and turned into a visage of granite. "I won't make you any promises that I can't—"

She raised her hand, resting her fingertips against his lips. "I don't want any."

"Then come with me." Aeddan took her by the hand, leading her into the darkened room.

"But what if someone—"

He stilled her words with a small shake of his head as he moved one arm up, so his finger slid over the flesh of her lips. She quivered with anticipation. "No one will know we are here."

He pulled his finger away, sliding it gently against her skin and down her chin. The flesh twitched below his teasing caress.

"*Aeddan...*"

He cupped her chin, raising it to his face. "This is for us."

He moved slowly, his gaze devouring while flickers of heat lapped at her skin, her breathing shallow. A thud and footsteps joined giggles in the hallway beyond, and her eyes flickered to the side, as if expecting someone to enter and find them.

"*Shh...* The door is locked." The whisper of his breath swept across her, sweet with the wine he had drunk earlier, and deep in the pit of her belly, the heat she'd tried to ignore swelled.

Her breath came in tiny puffs as he edged closer. Crowding her. But she wasn't scared or intimidated. She welcomed his closeness. Needed it and much more.

Elspeth's eyelids fluttered as the sensual promise of his kiss called to her. Their lips met and clung, his firm and warm. They pulled at her senses, and she gave in, welcoming the carnality as he devoured her. The thudding of her heart grew stronger, faster...heavier.

Sliding her arms around his broad shoulders, Elspeth skated her fingers over the light material of his jacket before reaching up to tangle in his slightly long hair. Without conscious thought, she pulled him closer, crushing her body against his hard frame. Desiring to find the passion she knew lay just beyond her touch.

The feel of him, his muscular body against her soft curves, left her gasping, and she pulled back just enough to allow herself to take a breath. The subtle scent of arousal wafted on the air.

"Skin against skin, heat to heat. Just imagine, Elspeth."

His languid drawl battered her, her mind clouding further, driving out the many arguments of why they shouldn't be here, doing this.

Aeddan's hands moved slowly, caressing over her almost bared shoulder. His fingers dragged across the small straps that held her bodice in position then burrowed in slightly, teased and touched before retreating. Licking flames of pleasure followed the careful caresses.

Who swayed, she couldn't say, but their mouths inexorably came back together. Aeddan clasped tight arms around her waist, the grip firm and sure. His hands moved so his thumbs could trace circles over her belly through the light material.

She closed her eyes and welcomed his careful touches. The touch was a mere glance but enough to set the pulsing desire dancing through her. His mouth roamed over her flesh, tracing along her jawline, and she inclined her head, angling up to allow him access to the sensitive skin beneath her ear.

Elspeth's knees turned to jelly as the sound of moans filled the air. She knew they were hers, but she couldn't stop them. She held onto him, like a life raft in the roiling seas. Senses adrift. She gulped down air as his fingers inched higher, finally cupping her breasts, the action scorching her through the layers of clothing.

"*Aeddan...*"

"Soon, my beauty." His whispered words left her shivering in reaction. The feel of the gaping gown was her first hint that he'd loosened the buttons at the back. "Let me see you. I need to feast my eyes on your creamy skin." Each word mesmerized her further.

The air was cooler now on her overheated skin, and she shivered, nipples puckering at the unexpected relief from the heat of the locked room as the heavy silk opened beneath his exploration and slid down. The gown hung from her elbows, and he slowly released her from its confines.

His fingers toyed with the demure edging of her corset cover, skimming over the lace and brushing against the skin he'd uncovered. Elspeth couldn't breathe as the now-familiar tug of want played at her senses. Splintering them until nothing but hunger remained.

"Aeddan?" The emotions swamped her, and she surrendered to the sensations. She forced her gaze to meet his. His eyes were slumberous, while his slashing cheekbones were crested with red. "Aeddan?"

"Elspeth, I want you. Do you understand what I'm saying?"

She nodded. She knew of desire. The maids had talked about it when they thought she was out of hearing, and lately, the uncomfortable feelings she'd been experiencing around him... She knew this was likely her only chance to experience it. She wanted to know the burn of passion.

She lifted shaky fingers to the tiny ribbon on her chemise, ready to remove the material barrier to her skin, but he stopped her. The touch of his hand on hers warm. Her body felt like it was melting in the darkened room. The sound of gaiety echoed from the other end of the large house.

"Not this time. Not like this." His words were a rasp.

Inside her, the molten liquid that had surged through her veins mere seconds before congealed. Became a lump in her belly. Confusion filled her. "You've changed your mind?"

He laughed, little more than a strangled bark of sound. "Oh, Elspeth, I haven't changed my mind. Not one bit." Then his mouth crashed down on hers.

*Bang! Bang!*

Startled, she reared back. "Someone's at the door!" She whispered, hoping he'd have some way of circumventing the scandal that could eventuate from the situation. She just knew they were about to be found and her gown was gaping open. Her fingers trembled as she fought with the material, heaving it back into place. Her cheeks burned, and she wanted the floor to open up and swallow her.

"Won't be a moment, Colonel." He looked at her, his expression grave, and he brushed away her fingers, slowly refastening the small buttons he'd just opened. "You're now thoroughly compromised. You do understand that?"

Her brain ceased to function. *Compromised?*

"Elspeth, we must marry now." In his eyes there was something she didn't understand. Whatever it was though, there was no anger. No frustration that his plans were thwarted.

Her stomach roiled. "But what about my plans?" Her cheeks flamed as she held her gown together.

"Major! What are you doing in there?" The muffled voice cut through the fraught atmosphere in the room.

"Just a minute, Colonel." He looked deeply into her eyes. "We can discuss this tomorrow. But accept me now."

"I..."

"Elspeth, say yes. We can work through the details later."

Surely it was wrong to want this without understanding all the factors? But she was compromised. The word that struck fear into any decent woman's heart. Heaven help her though, she wanted to say yes. *Oh God, it's so tempting.*

"But I..."

"Say yes, Elspeth. The rest is just details." His gaze captured hers, and she felt peace filling her.

"Yes, Aeddan. I will."

He smiled and took her arm, leading her to the locked door.

~

*T*he following morning Elspeth paced the floors of their rented house as she apprised Isabelle of the situation.

"You accepted him? But you barely know the man."

Isabelle's words didn't help Elspeth feel any better. Indeed, she felt worse than before. It was true. She didn't really know him, but he'd pressed her to accept him after they were caught in the library.

"Isabelle, I didn't exactly plan it." She headed to the window. "We were in a..." *How can I tell her I was compromised, willingly? This is my sister!*

"You did! You and he..." Isabelle's voice ended on an excited squeak. "What was it like?"

Elspeth turned, her skirts flying around her legs. "No! It wasn't like that! Oh, Isabelle, what have I done?" She slumped into a seat and covered her face with her hands. "I didn't want to get married. I was quite content with my lot in life."

The truth nagged at her. She really wasn't content. After all, she had once dreamed of a husband and family, but as the years passed that had gradually dimmed until the determined businesswoman had emerged. And then she'd stored away those other dreams—sure they'd never come to pass. When she'd finally accepted she'd never marry this happened.

"I didn't expect... Well, I certainly didn't imagine I'd receive a marriage proposal! We came to India to experience passion and to find out more about the interests of our suppliers and maybe find more. That was all." Elspeth clasped her hands together and squeezed them as she glanced at Isabelle, reclined on the chaise lounge.

"But what can you do about it then?"

"I don't... I don't think there is anything that can be done about it, Isabelle." That was the truth.

He'd said they would discuss the details later, but what would those details be? She'd promised herself to a man, one she suspected hid more truths about himself than he showed to others. What was he hiding from her though?

"Oh, Elspeth, I'm sorry. I shouldn't have pushed you into this plan in the first place. I just..." Isabelle's voice broke, and Elspeth shoved out of the chair, hurried across the room, then dropped down beside her sister, feeling dejected. She gripped Isabelle's hands.

"No, we both wanted this. But when one makes one's own bed...well, one must be prepared to lie in it." She inhaled deeply before patting her sister's hand. "So I believe the next thing I should do is write to Louisa and let her know of the development. At least...part of it."

Isabelle didn't look totally convinced. Elspeth was well aware of her disquiet, but there wasn't much else she could do right now, so she turned away.

The door opened, and Jacinthe entered the room. "Miss Forster, a note was just delivered from Major Fitzsimmons." She handed over the slip of paper, and Elspeth noted dimly how her hand shook as she took it. The writing was bold, slashing and heavy. Masculine.

She swallowed the exclamation of apprehension and turned the letter over, running her fingers over the red, waxed seal. Elspeth broke it with a crack. The paper crackled slightly as she unfolded it.

> *Elspeth,*
> *We have details to discuss. I will call on you*
> *   this afternoon and we can plan what*
> *   happens next. Until then, adieu.*
> *Yours,*

*Aeddan Fitzsimmons*

She breathed lightly, fancying she could catch a subtle waft of him on the paper. *Wishful thinking,* she told herself, but it didn't stop the way the blood in her veins thrummed or the heaviness that pooled in her belly.

"So? What does his note say?" Isabelle interrupted her moment of whimsy.

"What... Oh, he writes that he will be calling on me later today." She clutched the paper to her chest. "So I had best have some afternoon refreshments prepared." She hurried from the room, unwilling to face any more questions from her sister.

It was too *intimate.* After all, now it was no longer an academic discussion on what was missing. Instead she realized that it was soul baring. Something she didn't want to talk about with her sister.

She hastened to her room and opened her jewelry case, slipping the missive within it. She carefully smoothed out the paper before giving a sigh. What would become of them, she wondered. Would there be love along with the passion? Or would their union become like many other fashionable ones, where she furnished him with children and he went on his way once the initial heat cooled?

"I don't want a conventional marriage. I want more than just a home, husband, and children." Staring through the window, she closed her eyes and prayed, "Let this be the right decision."

She turned and shut the box on the letter and headed for the kitchen. They would need refreshments when Aeddan came to call.

# CHAPTER 9

*A*eddan prowled into the offices at Government House. The missive he'd received from his lordship had him nearly climbing the walls.

*Miss Forster needs protection. Plans are afoot.*
*Meet with me in my office forthwith. RBL*

Nothing else. His lordship was more than aware of the growing interest he had for Elspeth. In fact, it was almost more than that, but the exact *what* was undetermined yet.

He stopped at the desk, where Lytton's private secretary fixed him with his beaded eyes.

"His lordship has been waiting for you. Take a seat, and I'll apprise him of your arrival."

This time, though, Aeddan refused to take a seat. He watched as the man slipped within the office. Time was a factor right now, and he had no intention of wasting it. Not where Elspeth was concerned.

A fierce surge of possessiveness nearly overwhelmed him. That and concern. He'd sent Grundy to keep up surveillance on her house with strict instructions to inform him if anything unto-ward happened.

Grundy had smiled wryly before hotfooting it out of the house. He'd probably already heard tales of their emergence from the library. She'd been pink-cheeked and disheveled said some. Miss Forster had been distraught when they had left the locked room at the ball said another. Of course, Aeddan had lost no opportunity to spread the news of the betrothal. The grapevine didn't take long to kick into action when there was something juicy to report.

The door in front of him snapped open, and his lordship waited just beyond the opening. "Come in, Fitzsimmsons. We have things to discuss."

Aeddan wasn't pleased at the curt tone in Lytton's voice, but he followed him into his office. "You requested my presence?" He ignored the chair his lordship gestured to. He'd prefer to stand, nervous tension winding him tight.

"Yes. My wife indicated that after last night's indiscretion, you intend to wed Miss Forster. Is this correct?" Lytton grimaced slightly, and Aeddan was sure the man was sizing him up.

Aeddan nodded, noting the way Lytton held himself.

Lytton took a deep breath, and his bushy brows drew together. "Right, then. Miss Forster is important to the empire, both in terms of her shipping company, which carries much needed seeds and grains, and also as a carrier of intelligence. Some time ago, we became aware that there was an informer who was carrying tales to the Russians about our movements here. They worked out that we were using The Company to send highly sensitive information back to the Colonial Office."

"The East India Company?"

His lordship bowed slightly in response to his question.

"Then why..."

"We needed another method. One no one else knew of. One that wouldn't attract suspicion."

Aeddan held his breath. So the captains were acting as couriers for Lytton? "And Miss Forster is aware of this?" The muscles in his hand clenched as he fought to contain the concern that welled.

"No. It was all arranged with her father. After his death, the captains and we here in Government House saw no reason for the association to end. But other news coming out of the Afghan provinces is concerning. It seems someone has leaked the information that we use Miss Forster's ships to carry packets, and they have indicated an interest in her."

"That explains the attention of others then."

Lytton looked at him, a query in his gaze. "And?"

"And it was pure luck the colonel came looking for us. He'd received a message to find Miss Forster. They—the person looking for her—wished to meet with her privately. In the conservatory. Naturally, I explained I would escort her there, but when we arrived, no one was waiting."

"They ran." Lytton stayed quiet for a moment, no doubt running through the information in his head.

They'd gone for Elspeth. They'd shown more than an interest in her. That couldn't be allowed. They wouldn't get their hands on her. He'd do whatever it took to arrange her safety. And that of her sister as well.

"Have they indicated what kind of interest?" Aeddan asked.

Lytton spun on his heel, striding to the window, and the uncertainty in Aeddan grew. He waited in the silence, sure he couldn't possibly want to hear what was to come.

"I fear they may try again to abduct her," Lytton said. "Take her to Kabul and use her as a pawn or bargaining chip."

"No! I won't allow that." Every muscle in his body clenched tightly, including his now aching jaw.

"After last night, I was sure you felt that way. But Fitzsimmons, the longer she is here, the more dangerous it will become." Now his lordship looked him in the eye, the tails of his coat still swishing from his spin back toward him. "You were going to act as her guide during her tour of the weaving districts?"

Aeddan nodded, unable to speak as the rage invaded every inch of his body.

"Good. You need to arrange for guards no doubt. Or better yet, marry the woman and offer her the safety of your house. The sister too. If she's determined to continue her tour, then it will all be aboveboard. Simple for you to arrange."

Aeddan gave a short nod. "I don't feel it would be wise to share this intelligence."

Lytton's gaze was piercing. "No. Women don't understand about these things."

He didn't really like the plan that was being forced on him, but at short notice it seemed the best option. "And how soon do you..."

"Pop on over and see Dr. Johnson, the bishop. He'll set you up with a license. Get it done quickly, man. Before they can get to her." He held out a piece of paper he'd taken from his desk and scribbled on. "Give this to the clerics. It will gain you speedy access."

His nod was little more than a jerk as he accepted the missive. Elspeth's safety was paramount.

"If that's all?" He snarled the question at Lytton who raised an eyebrow.

"I believe that's enough."

"One request, sir."

Lytton grunted.

"Isabelle. When we go, Isabelle will need to remain here. She's not yet sufficiently recovered."

"I will make arrangements for the younger Miss Forster, Aeddan. Have no doubt. Now go."

With that, Aeddan whirled to face the door. He reached out, his hand grasping the knob as Lytton spoke once more.

"Good luck, Aeddan. I fear you may need it."

Aeddan left the building and strode outside, where the sun was shining brightly. The heavy thud of his heart reinforced the primitive emotions that spurred him on.

Nothing outwardly had changed, but deep within him a realignment of his priorities had taken place. *From bachelor to bridegroom*, he thought whimsically as he searched for a conveyance to take him to the cathedral.

For the first time, he gave thought to how his parents would react to his marriage. *To Elspeth.* They were more open-minded than most of their peers, but he felt more than a little concern, dragging her into a world she clearly had little experience in. Even though she was the daughter of a gentleman, she was not of noble birth.

"Needs must." The reassurance didn't make him feel better—the conflict he'd been battling for days rose once more. How was he supposed to understand this need that bubbled away? That and the sense of urgency telling him to protect her. She would be his bride and receive the protection of his name, but the emotional war he fought confused him further. Unable to settle the argument, he pushed it from his mind. He'd address that issue later.

He found a carriage and gave orders to proceed to St Paul's Cathedral. He could have walked the distance, but something inside said to be quick. The gnawing concern was building deep within his gut. *Hurry, hurry*, ran the refrain. So he had given in and watched the seething mass of people making way for the cab. They were within the grounds now, and heading up the long path. The clatter of cobbles beneath the wheels jarred him from his thoughts.

The carriage halted, and he vaulted down, handing the coachman some coin before heading for the building, the total of his focus now on securing the license. *On securing Elspeth*, he told himself. Aeddan entered the building, the cool, refreshing air clearing some of the noonday fog from his mind.

"Hello, my son. What can I do for you?" One of the clerics swept forward, his long, white cassock swishing over the floors. His face wreathed in a welcoming smile.

"I've come to see the bishop."

The man stopped, his eyes assessing him from behind metal-rimmed spectacles. The cleric frowned over his glasses. "I see. And that would be about?"

"I wish to obtain a special license." He waited, holding his ground under the smaller man's scrutiny.

"Ahh, I see. In order to meet the bishop, you will need to make an appointment. Let me..."

*Appointment be damned!* Somehow though, he managed to keep himself from hurling the epithet at the man. Aeddan's lips firmed as he held out the letter Lytton had granted him. "I believe this will expedite my appointment."

The man's eyebrows drew up, and he broke the wax seal. Whatever it contained drained any color from the man's face.

"Follow me, Major Fitzsimmons." The man walked toward a doorway at the head of the chapel, and Aeddan followed. They moved through into an antechamber beyond, and the cleric indicated a hard, wooden bench. "If you'll take a seat, I'll see the bishop immediately."

"I'd rather stand."

The cleric was clearly discomforted by his words, and he gave a jerky nod then withdrew to the room beyond.

Aeddan looked through the vaulted windows, the depiction of the saints soothing his ragged emotions. It was a reminder of home, of cool breezes and a time when life moved at a less frenetic pace. When danger didn't lurk on every street corner. He breathed deeply, the stillness and peace of the room filling him. It washed away the rage and fear that had built within him.

The squeak of the door opening captured his attention, and he turned. There, clad in his purple robes, was the bishop.

"Major Fitzsimmons, I have received the communiqué from

Lord Lytton. If you would please follow me?" The bishop beckoned within, and the cleric made his escape as the door closed quietly. An imposing wood desk filled the room, but the bishop merely leaned on it. "A special license?"

"Yes, Your Grace."

The man frowned, and Aeddan had the impression he wasn't so sure of granting it.

"It had been my intention to marry Miss Forster before all this rose." Maybe it had and maybe it hadn't, his conscience reminded him, but he refused to allow anything to get in his way.

The bishop nodded and headed to the pigeonholes, unerringly reaching for the papers he required, then opened a large tome which sat on his desk. "I will need all the details of both bride and groom."

Aeddan rattled off the information, watching as the bishop transcribed them, his script careful. Then he laid the parchment on the table and called for the cleric. He scurried in and accepted the payment of coin, nodded, then left again.

"The marriage..." He glanced at the bishop who watched him.

"Any priest can officiate."

The license was handed over wordlessly, and Aeddan started to thank the bishop who had continued his scrutiny, but then thought differently. Instead, he gave a bow and retreated from the room, moving swiftly, heading through the large structure and in the direction of the road. The piece of paper tucked carefully in the pocket of his jacket.

*Elspeth...* He needed to see Elspeth. He hailed the first cab that passed him, waiting for it to slow before climbing in and giving directions.

As her house appeared before him, he caught a glimpse of black. *Uniforms. Damn.* It was Fortescue and Albemarle leaving the house. A curl of some emotion he refused to name rose in his chest. He paid the driver and stepped from the carriage at the

portico. The sun beat down, hot and humid, and he ignored the
need to peel his jacket from his sweat-slicked body.

Jacinthe, Elspeth's young maid, opened the door with a smile.
"Major! I believe congratulations are in order." She accepted his
hat and ushered him into the parlor where the two women
waited.

His brief "thank you," was accepted with another smile and
he entered the room. Isabelle beamed broadly at him, while
Elspeth watched him in silence.

"Well, Major. I am pleased to see you here. Welcome."

"Why thank you, Miss Isabelle. If I may..."

Isabelle rose. "Of course, Major. I have some tasks to attend
to, so I shall leave you to it." She moved swiftly to the door, but
stopped, her hand on the brass knob. "Oh, and Major? You may
call me Isabelle." Then she was gone, with a tinkle of laughter
and the swish of silk skirts.

His advance into the room was slow. Steady. Measured.

Elspeth watched him, the calm façade marred only by the
narrowing of her eyes. "So, Major..."

"Aeddan."

She narrowed her eyes further at the correction. "Fine.
*Aeddan.*"

He sighed.

~

*E*lspeth watched him advance. Her natural balance was
off with all the changes surrounding her. Isabelle was
practically bouncing, her excitement at the coming nuptials
surprising Elspeth more than she ever would have expected. That
and the note he'd sent earlier left her unsure of herself.

This was not the way she would normally act.

He advanced, and Elspeth controlled her desire to back up.

His easy smile belayed the gravity of his gaze. "Elspeth, we need to talk."

Her breath whooshed out. *Talk? He wants to talk?* "What about?"

"Our wedding. Or..." He blushed slightly and turned away.

*He's changed his mind. Needs me to release him from this travesty of an engagement.* The contents of her stomach congealed. It seemed obvious that upon greater inspection he regretted his impulsive actions of the night before.

"I... I release you from our engagement." She spoke as clearly as she could. She ignored the pain in the region of her heart and expected him to accept and leave.

Instead, he turned back with a frown. A pregnant silence rose between them as he studied her, his gaze intent. "It's too late for that, Elspeth."

Her breath caught in her throat, and she lifted a hand a little way. "What do you mean, too late? We aren't yet married. No official announcement has been made."

The grin he turned in her direction burned her. "I have no intention of releasing you from our engagement. Indeed, I have obtained..."

She watched as his eyes twinkled, and she was captivated. The boyish good looks she noticed before entranced her. "You've obtained what?" A seed of suspicion took root. "A special license?" The words were little more than a whisper.

He nodded. "Yes. Now, there are reasons for choosing this option."

She clutched her stomach. Special licenses were usually reserved for early births and those who were ruined. The thought flittered and she cringed.

"But we haven't..." She clapped a shaking hand over her mouth. *We haven't been intimate* almost slipped out.

"No. We haven't acted inappropriately. Well, not totally. But I do have very good reasons." He slid his fingers around her arm, tugging gently. "Come sit beside me. We have many things to discuss."

She dropped into the chair gracelessly as she slipped from his grasp. His eyebrows curved up, and she blushed, then cursed her precipitous action under her breath. The look he bestowed on her was gentle, and Elspeth bit her lip and glanced away momentarily.

"So, what do you wish to discuss then?" She stared at him, aware the look was probably belligerent.

He had retreated to a chair and lounged indolently. "You wanted to know the details, I thought."

Elspeth sucked in an unsteady breath. "Family. Children. Dowry."

Aeddan's nod unnerved her. "Family. I want children. I have sisters and brothers... Both my parents are alive. Your dowry doesn't really matter to me, but I can have a contract drawn up to secure whatever portion is yours. We can make provision that it be held in trust for our daughters, if you wish."

*My dowry doesn't matter? Hold in trust for our daughters?* The thought ricocheted through her. "What do you mean it doesn't matter to you?"

"I have funds enough to ensure our comfort. Should you wish to continue running the shipping company, I will support your decision, but my own funds are not sparse."

She stared at him, for the first time taking in the expensive and well-fitted clothing he wore. The comfortable way they fitted him, and his own nonchalant disregard for them.

"I have enough to outfit you like a queen and any children we may have."

"Where will we live?" She could no longer contain her curiosity.

"I have a house here, in Calcutta, as well as my home in London and a small estate outside of Lichfield. It was my maternal grandfather's." He blinked, and for a moment she wondered just what he tried to hide from her. "There are other...aspects of my history that you need to be apprised of. My father..." He squirmed in his seat as if uncomfortable with what he was about to reveal.

She waved her hand, not wishing to push him when there had already been so many surprises to this day. "No, I don't need to know right now. If you are as well set up as you said, then my sister... She will have somewhere to reside?"

"Indeed she will, Elspeth. In the short term, while we are India, she will live with us at North Point. Then, on our way home—"

Elspeth shook her head. "We will be traveling to Shanghai first. Isabelle is particularly interested in the importation of jade to England. Our agents have already made contact with people." She expected him to argue, but he surprised her yet again with a short nod.

"Then we shall travel home via Shanghai."

It all seemed too easy. Where was the catch she could almost see?

"So you have plans to arrange the contracts when, exactly?" she asked.

"As soon as possible. Within the week would be best. You see, there's a further issue. One that is quite..." Aeddan shook his head, as if lost for words. "At some point your father entered negotiations with the Colonial Secretariat. The captains of the ships are carrying intelligence for the Viceroy back to England."

Shock coursed through her. *Carrying intelligence?*

"No. That absolutely cannot be right. I would know." Her voice shook. But of course, everything she'd learned of Aeddan told her it was quite possible that he spoke only the truth.

"No. Your father made it clear to the captains that under no circumstances were you to be apprised. After he died, the captains continued this role without informing you."

"But..."

"The Russians have learned of this. We think..." He looked away, sighed heavily, and his shoulders slumped. "There is someone within Government House feeding information to the Russians. They have decided that you would be a prize. If they hold you, then the captains will be forced to negotiate. That's why Captain Elliott left you here, in my care. The suddenness of his reloading is unusual, is it not? He's joining a squadron who are en route to Falmouth. They will escort him and the *Zephyr* safely home. Even now he carries information, strategic details, to the Admiralty."

Her stomach coiled with dread. "But why us? Why Forster shipping lines?"

Aeddan shook his head, and she had the feeling he was telling as much of the information as he felt she needed to know. What he'd already imparted left her reeling.

"The rest isn't important. All you need to know is that I intend to wed you as soon as can be arranged. I have a special license and—"

"No." Finally, a spurt of white-hot anger coursed through her veins. She stood, shaking out her skirts. Every movement was little more than a jerk, which told of her agitation. "I will not be pushed into marriage. No one could possibly wish to hurt me. I have no value to anyone other than myself and my family." Her eyes burned.

"Elspeth, don't be..." He held out a hand, as if to stop her from reacting.

"What? Absurd? Hysterical?" She drew herself up to her impressive-for-a-female height. "Do not patronize me, sir."

"Damn it, Elspeth, I'm not patronizing you. But you and your sister are in danger. The sooner we wed, the sooner I can ensure your safety, openly."

His words bit deep, drawing her to sudden stillness. What if he was right? If he was, then Isabelle was in jeopardy too. Isabelle was still recovering from the malarial illness. Elspeth had responsibilities, not just Isabelle, but also to those employed by Forster shipping.

She sat back down and faced him, heartily ashamed of her outburst. The sting of a blush rose as the final spike of adrenaline seeped away. "I do beg your pardon. Of course, you would be aware of these issues."

Aeddan watched her for a moment before no doubt coming to the realization that she had regained her equilibrium—but it was a tenuous grip.

Obviously satisfied, Aeddan rose to stride across the room and took the seat opposite her. "I also need to tell you about my family." He gazed at her with an unusual earnestness.

Elspeth extended her hand. "There is no need at this time. Tell me your plan."

He sighed but complied.

# CHAPTER 10

*T*he cathedral was cool and peaceful as the four made their way up the aisle. They'd traveled together in the carriage, Grundy sitting with the driver and Isabelle, Aeddan, and herself in the body of the carriage.

She twitched at the bodice of her gown as she'd done several times since dressing. The pale blue morning gown wasn't what she would have chosen to be wed in; the material clung to her body, making her itch under the noonday heat. She'd only had five days to prepare, so there hadn't been time to arrange a custom-made dress, and she had to make do with one of the gowns she already had on hand. This one was a winter gown, yet the lightest color she owned. But as with most of the preparations, it reinforced the furtive feeling.

"Stop that," Isabelle whispered in her ear, and Elspeth pulled her hand away, aware that her action had been noted.

She glanced in the direction of Aeddan. It amazed her that he wanted her for his wife when so many of the younger set were better suited to his role. Yet, if any of the embraces they'd shared were indicative, he was as interested in pursuing the passionate side of their relationship as she was. She tingled all over at the thought of the liberties he'd already taken—the touches and kisses.

"Stop fidgeting, Elspeth."

She started at Isabelle's words. *What am I thinking? And in a church?*

Aeddan had cleared the path to their wedding with a ruthless efficiency that she'd found unsurprising. He'd had a man draw up the nuptial contract with speed and ensured she'd had someone to act on her behalf. He'd spoken to the vicar, making the necessary arrangements so they could be wed today. It was under his direction that her household had been packed up, ready to move to his much larger home, the last boxes heading to North Point—a house she'd never yet seen—this morning.

He'd convinced Lady Manton that Isabelle should stay with her, taking Jacinthe as her personal maid, while Elspeth and Aeddan traveled into the wilds of India. Nothing was left to chance.

If he'd been somewhat distracted, she told herself, he was busy. The week had passed in a blur while she prepared for her new life. What small amount of household items they'd amassed had been deemed unnecessary, and had been bequeathed to the next inhabitant.

When he'd met them at the door, he'd presented her with a tiny bouquet of lilies. The romantic gesture surprised her.

His fingers slid around her arm, and she shook herself free of the reverie.

"It's time."

His whisper, so close to her ear, was intimate, and she gasped. Glancing in his direction, she noted the smokiness of his gaze. Perhaps he wasn't as unaffected as she thought.

The vicar waited for them at the end of the aisle, his black gown severe and unrelieved, but he smiled and welcomed them. She had a vague impression of kind blue eyes and white sideburns.

"Come, friends. We will complete the ceremony here." He indicated a side altar, and Aeddan nodded acceptance.

The vicar's words flittered through her mind like a bug crawling through congealing honey, while her mind skittered and danced as if it were a dream. She focused hard, listened, and answered the questions that would change her status from spinster to wife. It was only when she felt the slide of the ring on her finger that the sense of unreality faded away.

Aeddan looked into her eyes, and she was sure there was a flash of heat there.

"You may kiss your bride now."

She watched as his head dropped toward her, the soft whisper of his breath teasing her senses. Their lips touched, gentle and cautious. Warmth to warmth. She reached up and clutched the black cloth at his shoulder, steadying herself against the onslaught of hunger erupting.

The delicious warmth she now associated with Aeddan curled in her belly, and she moaned quietly as he pulled away. He gazed deeply into her eyes then stepped back.

"Congratulations, Elspeth."

She was enveloped in a hug from Isabelle. Her sister clutched her tightly, held for an instant, then released her. She watched, confusion filling her, as Isabelle turned to Aeddan. *My husband*, her mind supplied.

"And Aeddan. May I call you that?"

*My husband.* The thought stole her breath. Her husband...the one she hadn't expected to have.

She blinked as Grundy extended his hand. "Mistress." He smiled broadly, and she took the hand, accepting the small shake.

Aeddan turned away, pressing something into the vicar's hands before he placed her hand on his arm. "You are more than welcome to join us, Father, for the wedding breakfast."

The vicar shook his head, murmured a low "no thank you," then raised a hand in farewell.

With a grin, Aeddan pulled her back down the aisle to the doorway, where the sun shone. Outside, she blinked rapidly, blinded a little after the darkness within the cathedral.

"Where are we going?" she asked.

"I have arranged a luncheon at the hotel, then we will take Isabelle to Lady Manton's residence. I thought, since we will leave the day after tomorrow, you might wish to rest before we leave. I arranged for a day of quiet preparation, if that suits you."

Elspeth frowned. "But Isabelle's trunks..."

"Have already been delivered to Lady Manton's. She is expecting your sister."

She glanced at Isabelle who grinned at her. "Did you know about this?"

Isabelle patted her hand as they reached the waiting carriage. "Yes. It was all arranged yesterday. Besides, I thought you might appreciate a day or two to get to know each other without me."

Elspeth blushed. Get to know... Was that some euphemism for something else? Something intimate and to do with the marriage bed? She knew a little of that. At least as much as any well brought up young woman should know.

She accepted the touch of Aeddan's hand as he helped her into the carriage. Isabelle arranged herself in the seat opposite as he settled beside Elspeth, picking up her hand and carrying it to his mouth. The kiss was brief, more a caress, but it still sent shivers of awareness rippling through her.

Once Grundy took his seat, the driver clicked and the carriage surged forward. Elspeth had only a moment to think about how different this had been from the noisy celebrations of Louisa's nuptials and leave taking. This felt almost furtive and rushed, and she worked at banishing her dissatisfaction.

The luncheon was lavish, and Aeddan had even arranged a cake. She blushed with shame at the remembered thought of the differences between this wedding and Louisa's. He'd been kind and thoughtful, ensuring she had all the trimmings that could be arranged in such a short time. He'd even organized for it to be served in the small, private dining room.

The stories he told made Isabelle and her laugh, and her spirits rose. When the time came to rise she'd thrown off her concerns and allowed her husband to lead her through the door.

"Your carriage, wife."

She stopped short as he spoke.

"Oh my." Her stomach twitched at his words. "You've never said that to me before."

He leaned in. "You've never been my wife before." He spoke gravely, but there was a twinkle in his eyes.

"How true," she murmured.

Aeddan helped her into the carriage and then handed Isabelle in before once more settling into the corner.

~

*A*eddan ushered Elspeth up the steps of his house while she clutched his hand tight.

The knowledge that he hadn't fully disclosed his identity weighed heavily on him. Tonight, he promised himself, he would reveal the rest of his secrets. Right now, he wanted to bask in the knowledge that she was his. Safe from those who would try to steal her away. He shied from any knowledge of his own emotions though.

The time he'd spent planning with Lytton, ensuring her safety, had filled his mind in the last few days. His lordship had assured Aeddan that he had others who would clean out the vipers in the government nest while they were absent. All he had to do was take Elspeth away and keep her safe.

Yet he doubted that Lytton could clear any infiltrators with any degree of speed. They'd be away for maybe two months—it should be enough time. But these were people who had connections with the Russians and the subversive groups, including possibly the French. Who knew what information they'd already gleaned? What plans they'd set in place for Elspeth?

They reached the top of the steps, and he steered Elspeth right, along a corridor. The rooms at the end were his, and he tried to see it as she would. The pale walls and thick, lush carpeting were cooling and spoke of money.

He noted the way she shook a little, and he reminded himself that she had no one to prepare her for this. Surely, any gently reared young woman would find this situation overwhelming.

He reached for the knob and opened the door. It swung without a sound and led into her chamber. It smelt a little of beeswax and flowers. The slatted wooden shutters had been closed but the glass window panes stood open, so it was dim, but the shine of the mirrors and dressing table-set flashed from the flickering light of the lamps he'd ordered lit.

The large wood bed was hung with creamy nets, matching the curtains covering the windows; a gentle breeze blew, and they billowed.

"This is lovely." She stopped and glanced around the room, the silk of her gown moving slowly before gradually stilling.

"I'm glad it meets with your approval. Your dressing room is through here." He opened another door, this one painted white with gold leaf knobs, and she gasped. Her gowns were already hanging in neat order, shoes lining the floor and bonnets sitting above. He retreated, and she followed. "This door leads to my room."

She paled just a little. "Oh yes, of course."

He bowed slowly, watching her. "I will leave you for now. I believe a bath has been ordered, and the maid, Anara, will be in to help you shortly. She was employed by Miss Harlington, the sister of the previous tenant, before she left for England so is schooled in the needs of a lady."

With those words he slipped through the entrance to his rooms, leaving her alone. As the door closed, Aeddan stood there, sucking much needed breath into his lungs. Curiously, he found himself wishing she was there right now. Not beyond the wood that separated them. Slow movements had him removing his coat and shirt, grimacing at the stickiness of the weather.

He rang the bell, and Grundy hurried in. "A bath, I think."

Grundy nodded. "Yes, Major. When would you like dinner to be served and where?"

"I think just after seven in the dining room, then send everyone off for the night. I doubt we will need anyone."

"Anara has already organized a bath for Her—"

"No. Don't say it."

Grundy gave him a questioning look.

"No, I haven't told her yet." The vague uneasiness that had been dogging him over the last few days re-emerged.

"You're going to have to tell her soon, Major. Don't want her to find out from someone else." Grundy spoke sternly, and Aeddan nodded.

"Tonight. I'll tell her tonight." He pulled his fingers though his hair, knowing Grundy was watching him. On a sigh, he admitted, "I didn't want her to have any reason not to marry me." It was a truth he'd avoided until now, but Grundy seemed even more unnerved by the admission than he was.

"Major—"

"Grundy, just organize the bath." He turned away. Rarely did he cut his man off, but right now he didn't want to deal with the questions. "And inform Anara to tell my wife dinner will be at seven."

The bath cooled his body but not his mind, and when Grundy laid out his clothes, he was pleased to have his man fully employed, not questioning his actions. Aeddan checked the clock on the mantel: a quarter to six. He had time to head down to his library and finish his letter to his parents.

# CHAPTER 11

*T*he letter was shorter than he wanted, but to be honest, he couldn't think of any way to explain to his parents about the woman he'd married without causing them concern. So he'd kept it brief.

> *Dear sir,*
> *I am delighted to inform you that this morning*
> *I took a wife. Elspeth and I said our vows*
> *in the Cathedral of Calcutta. She is of good*
> *birth, and is the daughter of a gentleman,*
> *Mr. Joseph Forster, Esq, late of Port Isaac,*
> *and Judith Forster, nee Underland-Beavis.*
> *It is to be hoped that I shall soon be making my*
> *way home, as I have undertaken one final*
> *mission for the Admiralty and will be*
> *escorting my wife and her sister back to*
> *England via Shanghai.*
> *In due course, I will instruct my wife to write*
> *to Mama.*

*Your obedient son,*
*Aeddan Fitzsimmons*

He glanced at the missive on the desk, wondering again how his family would react to the news.

Aeddan frowned. It was five minutes to seven. *Where is Elspeth?* He stood, stretching his cramped muscles.

Then, with a quick, "to hell with it all," he headed into the hall. As the door shut behind him he looked up, and his breath caught in his throat. His wife was descending the stairs, her hair coiled and curled on the top of her head, with flowers pinned into the side. Her gown was a pale green wonder that molded to her form, accentuating her height and her bountiful breasts.

"Sir."

She reached out her hand and he grasped it, grateful for the unseasonal heat which masked his reaction to her; the way his body hardened and his breath came faster. His skin prickled as desire rolled through him.

"You look quite ravishing."

His Elspeth blushed, the fine shake of nerves evident in the fluttering of her fingers.

"Come, let us go to the dining room."

They moved slowly, in rhythm. Their every movement attuned. It was as if they knew that soon they would be joined as one in the oldest dance of all. He gulped down the response that rose instinctively.

The table was laid, ready with a cold selection. "I thought a collation might be welcome this evening."

She turned. "Yes, a wonderful idea. After all, lunch was such an elaborate affair."

He winced, momentarily unsure if his choices had been wise. "You would have preferred..."

"Oh, it was perfect, Aeddan. You made the day lovely. Thank you." As she spoke, she dipped her head.

Pride bloomed. "Then it was my pleasure, Elspeth." He led her to the chair and waited as she made herself comfortable, then took the seat beside her. "Now, what would you like to begin with?"

She chose carefully, a mixture of meats and lighter salad vegetables. As they ate, they talked of the political situation in England, the many places he'd seen during his time with the army, and lastly of traveling. He once more found himself surprised at the breadth of her knowledge.

Grundy cleared away as they finished their main course, and then he returned with a platter of fresh fruits and cool, refreshing wine. As he started to pour Aeddan shook his head. "No. I'll see to that. You may go."

Aeddan poured a glass for both of them and watched as she sipped cautiously. "How lovely and light."

"French. I imported several cases last year for my personal use. I think tonight counts as a special event though, don't you?"

She blushed again, and they continued talking.

Finally, he rose and she took his proffered hand. "We should retire."

Elspeth stared at him as he scooped up the bottle by the neck. "Come."

At the foot of the stairs he stopped and allowed her to make her way up before him, noting the sway of her hips beneath the silk gown. He wanted to growl.

As the night had worn on, he'd watched her. She was animated when speaking, without any of the uncertainty that had irritated him in so many of the misses he'd squired in the past. He'd chosen well.

They moved down the corridor. At her room he stopped her. "I'll see you soon."

She blinked and opened the door, then was gone from sight. He exhaled heavily, catching the faint waft of aromatic spices on the air. He went to his own room, placing the wine on the small table, together with the glasses he'd palmed earlier. He poured some and dimly noted the tiny tremor of his hand. He'd need every scrap of control for the night ahead.

The chamber was organized as he'd instructed. The doors to the balcony stood open, and a fitful breeze stirred the lacy curtains. A bottle of aromatic oils sat on a bedside table, and scented candles placed around the room flickered invitingly. Floral tributes filled the sides, their lush, rich fragrance mixing with that of the candles. It was a space ripe for worshiping at the altar of passion and sensuality.

Tonight would certainly be a night for her to remember. He'd planned to introduce her to pleasure, to the give and take of sexuality.

It was counterpoint to his personal studies, with the careful crafting of the environment and her innocence, but for now, she'd need to be prepared before he could begin schooling her. If she was amenable to his plans, he thought with uncharacteristic concern.

Quick strides took him to his dressing room and he moved with speed now, jerking his clothes free from his body, allowing the cool air to caress his skin. A cloth and basin of water waited for him, and he took the moment, wiping his body in the heady atmosphere. His erection jerked.

Finished, Aeddan sighed as he slid on his bedroom robe and knotted it carefully. The feel of the cloth sliding over his naked flesh was sensual. The fine rasp over his sensitized skin left him with the feeling of nerves coiling as the churning need in his belly grew more insistent.

"She's a virgin, Aeddan. You need to be careful." With those words, he left the dressing room, knowing that she'd be waiting beyond in her bedroom. Unable to contain himself any longer, he stepped up to the door, gave a single rap, then strode into her chamber.

Elspeth's bedroom was also lit by candlelight, the glow flickering in the breeze. She stood, looking at the floor, her arms wound around her body, as if nervous about him seeing her and what was to come. Her discarded gown had been replaced by the night-rail he'd ordered for her. The material of her gown was thin. He could see the shadows and dips of her body through the lacey material of her wrapper.

"You're beautiful, Elspeth."

With a jerk, she raised her head, and he noted the blush that glowed on her cheeks. Her gaze drifted down then skittered away. "Aeddan... I..."

He smiled, understanding what she couldn't say, and took her hand. "We'll go slowly. I want you to enjoy tonight."

His own mind skittered at the sight before him. Never before had he seen so beautiful a woman. He wondered at the zing of anticipation that filled him. As their lips met, he fought his body for control.

Their lips clung, warm and soft. He nibbled carefully, unwilling to scare her. The realization that she would need tutoring had come to him days ago. A sensualist such as himself couldn't expect her to grasp the significance of his needs. Not yet. But soon, if he didn't miss the way she was already reacting to his touch, she would understand. Hopefully, she'd become a willing participant too. She was a woman of fire, just what he needed, rather than some cold, unfeeling girl.

A moan filled the air as he deepened the kiss and Elspeth's mouth opened beneath his. Pleasure suffused him. He'd taught her this. Her response was shy as she slid her tongue into his mouth, just as he'd shown her during the week. He had to suppress the shudder that worked through him.

On a groan, he pulled back, filling his lungs deeply, while gripping the fingers of one hand. Her scent filled his mind.

"Come." Aeddan tugged her in the direction of his own room,

walking backward, waiting for her reaction as she entered the haven he'd created for them.

Elspeth's eyes widened as she stepped into the chamber. "Oh my!" Her breathy words made him smile.

"For you... All for you." Then he tugged her into his arms, his mouth descending once more.

~

*A*ny and all sensible thoughts fled from her mind. His hands settled around her waist and tugged her close while his mouth feasted on hers. She opened to his invasion, glorying in the warmth that filled her. Her body softened, giving into the languor that spread through her. Between her legs, an emptiness, she now understood as *need*, pulsed.

He nibbled at her bottom lip before tracing her jawline. "So beautiful," he murmured, and she shuddered at his words.

Nerves jumped beneath his touches as each move left her breathless. She splayed her fingers on his broad shoulders, noting the hardness beneath his bedroom robe. It gaped, and she caught sight of bronzed flesh.

With great trepidation, she let her arms slide down his chest, gripping the deep lapels with an unsteady hand. She wanted to see more of what lay beneath the cloth. "Aeddan? Take it off for me."

He pulled back. "Not yet."

"Why not?" She wanted to feel the flesh she'd glimpsed up close.

"Because..." He stopped and sucked in a deep breath. "Not yet. Trust me."

"But..."

"For an innocent, you're mighty hurried, wife."

His words left her speechless. *Am I too forward?*

She must have looked worried, because he frowned. "You

haven't any experience. If I don't do this right, you won't enjoy it. It will probably even hurt."

She'd heard of that, but the hunger to know more beat at her. *How could such pleasure hurt?* That made no sense. The maids had also talked of pleasure, and she was sure their experiences were mere facsimiles of what she was experiencing. "So..."

"Trust me." He leaned in again, touching his forehead to hers, and she inhaled deeply, but her mind spun as the very essence of him overwhelmed her.

She gave up any modicum of control. "Fine. Then teach me. Teach me everything."

As if those were the words he needed to hear, he pushed her slightly so she reclined almost against the wall. The grace she had seen before stripped away as he once again set his mouth to hers.

The kiss was deep. Seductive. It stole her senses while his hands roamed over her body, harder and firmer than before, but he didn't scare her, even when they settled at her breasts, molding over her curves, and she arched into his touch. When he caressed her nipples her breath caught and down below her body quivered in reaction.

This time when he pulled back, his eyes glittered. "Let's get this off you."

He hooked his hands under the lacy confection of her wrap, and it slid to the floor, forgotten. The darkness outside settled, yet inside the room was illuminated by the candles, the light reflecting off the mirrors and crystal vases.

In the mirror in her own room, Elspeth had noted the way the lace gown she wore hid very little. It was held together with four tiny buttons. Her hands itched to hold the gown together, in place, but she fought and conquered the impulse.

He settled his fingers on the top button, and she gasped. "Aeddan..." Her unspoken question made him smile for some reason.

One button popped free, then another. She stood still, letting him release the tiny pearls, while her body felt as if it melted beneath his touch. Heat pooled between her legs, and her nipples tightened into wicked buds of need, such as she'd never before experienced. The lace bedeviled her, and she moaned with each move.

Finally, looking pleased with himself, Aeddan pushed the gown from her shoulders. She gasped as the cool air caressed her overheated skin. She held her legs together, hoping to assuage the emptiness she felt, but it didn't work.

"Aeddan?" The throb increased deep inside her body.

His hands moved to the knotted belt at his waist, his eyes hooded. Her mouth dried as the tie gave way and the robe fell open. On a careless shrug, it dropped away and pooled next to her gown.

She'd never seen a naked man before, and her startled gaze zeroed in on his hard, long length before she gasped. He smiled as she looked her fill.

"How is *that* going to fit?"

He laughed, a chesty rumble that made her nerves spike and jump. "Have no fear. It will."

She swallowed; for an instant she knew fear. "If you say so." She had her doubts.

Aeddan took her hand and led her to the bed. At the edge, she sank down but he didn't follow.

"Aren't you..."

He shook his head. "Not yet." Instead, he reached for a tiny decanter at the table and poured some of the contents into his hand. "Let me pleasure you first."

His eyes almost smoked, and she swallowed, unsure how to react.

"Lie back and relax."

She followed his instructions, and the soft fabric cradled her body. No one, not even her maid, had seen her like this since she'd been a babe. Coherent thought was difficult. *Don't let me embarrass him or me!*

The spicy aroma caught her attention as he laid his hands on the skin of her stomach; the touch left her muscles tensing. He moved his hands slowly, and she arched, feeling the quivering in her belly, as he rubbed the oil over her skin.

*Such pleasure!* No one had told her of this.

His hands found her ribcage and she moaned a little, each pass moving higher until finally caressing the edges of her breasts. She moved and squirmed, uncaring now of anything except the hunger that gnawed at her while her blood heated.

"*Aeddan?*"

"Soon, Elspeth," he growled as his touch grew bolder, swiping over her breast with slow, gentle caresses. His fingertips found and lingered at her budded nipples.

Her body fought for control of her mind while the ache between her legs grew. Now her fingers twined in the covers of the bed.

He kept up the ministrations. Sliding his fingertips up over her shoulders, he smoothed before pulling away. She drew in a ragged breath and opened her eyes to watch him pour more oil into his cupped palm.

"Let me."

When he turned back, his face was tight. "Not yet, little one."

The smile he bestowed on her was hot as he set his hands on the top of her thighs. This time she cried out, and his smile became darker. *Wolfish.*

The tightness in her chest took her by surprise, and by the time he'd found his way to her most intimate flesh she was panting and writhing with hunger and need.

He climbed onto the bed, towering over her as he slipped one careful finger between her legs. "*Pleasure.* Lovemaking is pleasure. One I want you to share with me."

Unable to form a coherent word, she rested her gaze on him.

He teased the folds between her legs, and she couldn't help but watch, mesmerized.

Each time he glanced the bud of her clitoris she cried out. Then he pushed his finger deeply within the warm channel between her legs. She shuddered, her body reacting without any conscious thought. Pressure built. Arousal, hot and sharp, speared her, but she didn't know what to do.

"Aeddan?" Her voice was thready, and he dipped in to kiss her lips.

Rapaciously, he fed from her. His urgent movements married with the motions of his hand, and she undulated, unable to remain still, tension coiling in her belly, her body straining for something just out of reach. Sliding his finger, he toyed until some desperate peak of pleasure seemed within her grasp.

This time when he pulled away and slid his hand from her, the hunger had her reaching for him.

"Aeddan? Did I do..."

"Hush, my love."

He shifted, chest bellowing in and out, as if searching for some restraint. The ticking of a clock filled the air. Once, twice, and a third time, before he lifted his head, his gaze harsh.

"Now."

She couldn't pull away from his searching look, and his voice was guttural.

Slowly, achingly slow, he lifted her hips, reaching for a pillow, which he slipped under her derriere. She parted her legs, and he kneeled between them.

"There will be pain."

The words came from far away, and she couldn't focus as her body clamored for something just beyond her reach.

She noted the way his teeth were gritted, and he ran an oiled hand over his erect shaft. All she wanted now was him.

Elspeth wasn't sure what she needed, only that he knew and held the key to the release she knew was close. "Aeddan? Please."

One more rub between her legs left her moaning and flinging her back with the sensual haze. He fitted himself to her core and pushed. The barrier gave and she keened at the sharp pain. Her body stiffened as he held still within her.

Tears leaked from between tightly closed eyes. She took one breath then another while she looked up at him. He'd told her there'd be pain. But somehow, she hadn't understood.

He didn't move, still deeply embedded within her. She could feel him, damn him! Her body reacted to the burning sensation, seeking to end it. When she would have pulled away, he placed a hand on her tummy. "Be still."

Around his lips was bone white as if he too shared her pain.

"Aeddan?" The sting was receding, but there was still a stretching and overfull sensation. "I don't..."

"Never. Again. I. Promise." His chest bellowed, and he held still a little longer. "No more pain now, my love." Elspeth tried to pull away again, but he caught her with hard fingers. "Wait."

So she did. At last the burn retreated, and she relaxed. "Will it always be like this?"

"No. Now there will be pleasure. Only pleasure between us."

He nudged her with his hips, and she waited for the pain she was sure would follow his moves. But there wasn't any—just the erotic sensation of friction. He shifted again, and this time she gasped. Her body betraying her totally with a dizzying pleasure.

Again he nudged, and she unconsciously mirrored his moves, meeting him. Each successive thrust faster and deeper than the last as they moved in swift unison. Sounds of slapping flesh and the scent of arousal filled the air.

Her body demanded release from the wicked, driving hunger. She didn't know how, only that the release of the driving hunger was with him.

"Aeddan?" She keened and he grunted.

"Let go. Give in to the pleasure."

Unable to help herself, she did, and her body splintered as he pounded into her, over and over again. She cried out, arched, and he joined her, stiffened against her.

For a moment there was nothing. Just a whirling vortex of gratification, then she fell, closing her eyes and giving in to exhaustion.

# CHAPTER 12

*A*eddan stared at the ceiling. Elspeth slept heavily, and he frowned, his arm flung over his head. *What the hell happened here tonight?* He'd planned to give her pleasure, but the cataclysmic orgasm stunned him. He'd never lost his head like that.

He damned himself for the secrets he kept from her. He hadn't told her who he was either. *How the hell do I tell her?*

She snuffled in her sleep, a delightful sound that made him feel even angrier with himself. He slid his hand over her naked back, loving the silky feel of her.

"Elspeth."

"Who..." Her groggy word made him smile.

"It's me. Aeddan. I need to talk to you."

The sudden stillness, the way her muscles tensed, told him she realized she was naked in his bed. He slid out of the bed and grabbed her robe along with the two glasses of wine. She turned over, clutching the sheet against her chest, as he held the glass out.

He couldn't contain the laugh. "I've seen all of you, so there's no need to hide."

She blushed deeply, accepting the goblet as he dropped the robe on her lap. Her eyes widened and her face flamed before she turned away. He told himself firmly she'd been innocent until tonight so that made his teasing unfair.

Moving to the end of the bed, balancing the drink in his hands, he scooped up his bedroom robe and donned it while she hurriedly placed her drink on the side table and struggled into the lacy confection. He did wonder if she realized it didn't hide anything. Wisely, he kept silent and made his way back onto the bed, slipping under the covers in the chilled night air.

"Well..." She glanced in his direction then away.

"Yes. So... Uh.. You feel fine?" He cursed his ham-handed words, but how the hell was he supposed to open this discussion? After all, he'd just deflowered his first virgin. The fact that she was his wife made him even more uncertain.

"Uh, yes. Thank you." She blushed a deeper scarlet, and he sipped his wine while sorting through his scattered wits.

He dragged her close against him. For a moment she stiffened but then nestled into his caress. With one hand, he rubbed her through the light lace covering and wished he could make the truths he was about to speak just disappear.

"I need to tell you something. Something I should have told you before."

She turned in his direction, and a curl dropped from her now less than perfect hairstyle.

"I'm rather more than I explained previously."

Elspeth watched him, and he was glad for her silence.

"My father is an earl. I also have a title. I'm the Viscount Traughton, and my father is the Earl of Carrington. That makes you the viscountess."

She gasped, spilling a little wine on the sheets then batting at the drips with an ineffectual hand. "What? No, see, that can't possibly be correct. If it were, then you wouldn't have married me." Her face turned pale, and she bit her bottom lip.

He shook his head, noting the way her hands trembled. "It's true. I am Aeddan Fitzsimmons, but I have all the extra titles that go with it."

As he watched, she blanched further and shook her head. "You tricked me... Knew that our marriage would be—"

"No, I didn't trick you. I omitted some facts, but I never lied, Elspeth."

She hmphed and looked away. "How am I supposed to find my place in your world when I'm not even from the same..." She sighed deeply, visibly upset by his revelation. "I'm not even from the same social set as you. I don't know how a viscountess is supposed to behave."

She looked so miserable and woebegone. The tears welling in her eyes had him wanting to gather her in his arms, but right now there was a chasm between them. One that hadn't existed earlier in the evening. He had to breach it and quickly.

"We'll get through this together, Elspeth. I'll be there to support you."

She glanced away before snorting inelegantly. "That's fine in some places, but not everywhere. You know that." She shook her head, tears tracking down her face, and she rubbed at the glistening trails. "It's too late now. You should have told me. Given me a choice."

Her bitter words wounded him deeply, but she was right. He wouldn't be able to be there all the time. And it was too late. Much too late. Now all he could do was try to rectify the situation he'd created.

She pushed at the bedcovers, slid the glass onto the small bedside table, and crawled out of the bed.

"Where are you going, Elspeth?"

She barely glanced at him, her face stiff. "I'm going to my bedroom."

"Why?"

She stilled and settled a look on him that questioned his sanity. "Because that's how married couples sleep."

He smiled. "Not all. Now, please come back here."

She gasped and looked at him. "But Aeddan, won't your staff be..."

He grinned. "Not at all. And if you go in there, I'll have to follow. I'm rather comfortable here though, and I fancy that bed will be too short and small for both of us."

With a long sigh and flaming cheeks, she headed back to the bed.

"Just a minute!" He pulled off the top sheet. "It might make you more comfortable." She hadn't bled, but she'd feel more comfortable on the fresh sheet below.

She looked away as he balled up the material he'd removed and shoved it into his dressing room. It could be dealt with in the morning.

Without casting a glance at him, she crawled into the bed. He opened his arms, and she swung around and eyed him with suspicion before she scooted closer. He drew in the scent of her and hauled her against him. She settled and her breathing slowed as she gave into sleep. But he lay awake for a long time.

$$\sim$$

*A*s she descended the stairs, Elspeth patted her hair. Waking in his bed had left her feeling rather...*strange*. When she combined that with the curiously empty throb between her legs and the achy tingle, she felt her equilibrium was severely compromised. None of the maids at home had mentioned any of these things. She shook her head, hoping to clear the miasma clouding her mind.

Aeddan had already risen when she woke, so at least she was spared the indignity of not knowing how to react under the circumstances. She knew he'd held her in the night, their naked bodies entwined. But still... She gulped down an unsteady gasp. Husbands and wives weren't supposed to sleep together. It was against the natural order of their social set.

The bottom of the steps loomed, and she stopped, steadying herself against the post before she made her way toward the doors of the dining room. As she opened them and peered within, she noted Aeddan—her husband—waiting for her.

"Good morning, Elspeth." His voice was deep, and the secret places within her body started quivering with anticipation.

She blushed hotly at the twinkle in his eye, while she fought to regain her composure. "Good morning, Aeddan... I mean... My—"

He shook his head. "No. Not now, Elspeth." He frowned heavily, and she bit her lip.

"But..."

He shook his head again, and she faltered. *What have I said wrong?* Then the thought came on swift wings. *He doesn't want anyone to know about his title?*

He beckoned her to the seat beside him. "Come sit down, wife. Then we can break our fast together." He'd been reading the paper, but now folded the sheets and laid them aside.

Elspeth reached for the teapot and poured some of the fragrant liquid into her cup.

"Did you sleep well?"

The pot clattered in her hands. *How am I supposed to answer that?* "Very well, thank you, husband."

A maid entered the room, bearing a tray, and started laying the foods on the buffet beside the table. Bacon, eggs, and even kippers sat alongside toast and varied conserves. She watched with wide eyes as they cluttered the side. Next to the warm foods sat a large bowl of fruit, the greens, yellows, and golds catching her eye.

Aeddan rose and indicated she should join him. Amazement filled her as he mounded food on his plate. It was piled high, a veritable mountain of mushrooms and tomatoes, along with a variety of meats. Her own stomach churned just a little, and she decided on toast, with a dark yellow conserve, and grabbed a banana and mango; some of the foods she'd only sampled since her arrival, others remained a mystery still.

Aeddan eyed her plate. "Is that enough?"

She smiled. "It is for me."

They both reclaimed their seats, and for a while there was silence as the two of them ate in companionable silence. Her mind skipped and danced as memories of the night before crowded in.

When she lifted the mango he put down his knife and fork and speared her with a look.

"What?"

He smiled. "Nothing. I was just wondering how you plan on eating that." He pointed to the fruit she held in her hand, the sticky juice oozing slightly on her hands.

With a deep blush, Elspeth ducked her head. "I'm not entirely sure. But it looks and smells so good."

When Aeddan held out his hand for the firm, orange fruit, she passed it over and watched as he deftly sliced the skin into quarters, all the way through to the large seed within. Next he cut off some of the juicy, orange flesh and held it out.

Elspeth held out her hand, but he shook his head.

"Open wide."

Startled, Elspeth opened her mouth, and he slid the juicy piece within her mouth. Pulpy liquid dribbled down his hand, but what mesmerized her was the look in his eyes. *Hungry.* His eyes shone with need. Just as they had the night before.

Without conscious thought, she swallowed then leaned forward and licked the rivulets of gold staining his skin. He groaned, the sound echoing through the silent room, and he captured her gaze. Held it prisoner to his will.

Not breaking contact, he raised another sliver of flesh and

held it out. She opened her mouth, and this time he took his time sliding it between her lips. She swallowed, her body burning with a dark, sensual hunger. She licked at his finger, her tongue rasping over his skin, snaking down to his wrist, following the liquid trails.

Aeddan pulled his hand away, a shocked look settling on his face. Wordlessly, he moved forward and fitted his lips to hers. The connection between them was as explosive as wildfire. Sensations rippled through her, stealing both her senses and her breath. It was a blazing fire in need of quenching, and only he could douse the flames. His lips moved, ruthlessly, claiming what was his, and she gloried in it.

Firm hands tugged her out of her chair, and she gave into his demands. He settled her in his lap, his arms holding her close as she slipped her fingers into his hair. The kiss deepened and tongues tangled in her mouth.

*Knock!*

Face flaming, she tugged away and nearly fell from his lap. His hands held her in place as she gasped, hoping to settle the jittering emotions fighting within her body.

"Come in!" Aeddan's roared words surprised her, and she stood, then straightened her skirts.

A small maid scurried in and started clearing away in silence, but Elspeth noticed the way the girl averted her eyes from them. Elspeth resumed her seat and drank deeply of her now cooled tea, waiting for the door to shut once more.

"So, what plans do you have for today?" She fitted her hand over her belly, certain she was once more under control.

His wolfish smile set her veins humming once more. "I have many plans. But the first one is to find a suitable mount for you."

She gasped, and he smiled.

"Sirrah! Just what do you..."

She'd heard the stable boys talking like that and knew exactly what the word *mount* meant.

He grinned broadly. "A horse, Elspeth. You will need a horse of your own."

She subsided with a gulp as her face flamed once again. *What has he done to me?* But the truth was there, he'd opened her eyes to the pleasures of the flesh.

He leaned back, a small smile playing on his full, sensuous lips. "But yes. I have that in mind as well." His eyes became grave under her gaze. "I am... I would consider myself a sensualist. So the pleasures we have shared are merely the beginning, Elspeth. I want to share that and more with you. To open your eyes to a world of such pleasure that you never would have experienced. To share it with you. Only with you."

Breathing became almost impossible as if some great blockage had settled in her chest, stopping her from drawing enough oxygen into her starved lungs. His words sank in, while her mind whirledThere was more? What they had shared was a mere beginning and one he would share only with her? Her mind clamored that last night had been unimaginably...satisfying. Her beleaguered mind struggled to find a more appropriate word choice given the subject matter.

"I..." She opened her mouth and closed it again as he laid his hands on hers.

"I'll never do something that makes you uncomfortable. But pleasure and its pursuit are skills I have actively sought. I want to share that with you, Elspeth."

She gave a small nod. What else could she do? She'd need to ponder on this though, she told herself firmly as she stood up.

"Where do you wish to seek a horse?"

He smiled, obviously aware that she felt at sea, then named the markets. He eyed her dress critically. "You'll need to change, though I find that gown most alluring." He gave another wolfish grin. "I could come and help you."

She scurried for the door. "I'll be done as quickly as possible." She fled the room to his bark of laughter.

~

*T*he following morning they rose early, and he watched as Elspeth dressed in the dim, predawn light. She'd been scandalized that he'd expected her to ride dressed like that, but he'd shushed her, telling her, *"In case we need to move quickly."*

She'd made a sexy, little moue with her lips, and heaven help him, it had taken all his willpower to ignore it. To walk away and not touch her.

He'd chosen a frisky, white Arabian mare for Elspeth and had been adamant that before he took consignment, she had to show that she could handle the horse. Of course, Elspeth had more than proved her mettle in both the side saddle and astride.

Riding astride had been under duress, but once she was in control of the reins, her face had shone with pleasure. *"Why, it's so much easier to control her!"*

He'd smiled at her enthusiastic response as she crooned to the animal. The horse had pranced, but she had brought the horse back under control with gentle yet firm commands.

Now comforted that she was more than capable, he watched as she belted in the pants he'd purchased for her.

"It feels so odd, Aeddan. I just hope no one sees me." Her long hair was fastened back in an utilitarian plait, which she'd fashioned into a bun high on her head, and the white shirt he'd insisted she wear molded to her figure.

Lust thickened his tongue, along with other aspects of his body, before he pressed the dun-colored leather jacket into her hands. "Put this on."

She gave him a questioning look then shrugged into it. It subdued her natural femininity, but nothing could hide the fine features of her face or the long neck that screamed *woman*.

They made their way down the stairs, where his man waited with refreshments. "Drink and eat now, and we'll be on our way. We will stop later in the day to break our fast properly."

Elspeth followed his instructions, drinking the bitter coffee and nibbling at the pastry she'd accepted, finishing both in silence. Then, swinging her hat onto her head and tying it in place, he gave her one last, long look and nodded. Together they left the house, though he noted the longing look she cast at the building.

"We'll be back soon enough."

At the bottom of the steps outside the front door, his men waited, most of them already in the saddle, and he herded her over to *Sana Zahrah*, her horse. With a quiet boost, he hoisted her into the saddle, then his man brought his around, the big-chested Waler he'd purchased on arrival in India.

*Devil's Chaos* was in a tetchy mood. He sidestepped and snorted, but *Sana* acted like a lady. He marveled at how calm and quiet she was, and congratulated himself on the choice again. The traits might just help keep Elspeth alive if there were any incursions by the locals.

Elspeth held her reins with just the right touch, sitting high in the saddle, and smiled. "Well then, I believe I'm ready."

With a last look around, he nodded and clicked his tongue. The horse surged forward, muscles bunched tightly, as if knowing that a long journey lay ahead and he was keen to begin.

Elspeth brought her horse alongside, as they'd agreed the night before. "How many hours do you expect to travel today?"

He squinted, eyes on the horizon. "Maybe eight to ten, depending on how far we can get. From here we are traveling to Barasat."

She raised a hand and squinted into the distance. "Did we set off so early because of the temperatures?"

"That, and we can get further and take breaks in the middle of the day."

Elspeth nodded soberly as they trotted through the city. It was quiet to look at, but he knew it was a seething mass below the surface, rather like the political situation. In his pocket he carried letters from Lytton to the many officials, in whose cities they would travel. They offered protection as well as introduction. The cities were the least of his concerns.

No, if there was any attempt to abduct Miss Forster—*his wife*, he corrected himself firmly—they would take place in the unprotected areas. Most likely at night, while they were encamped. He gripped the leather reins in his hands. "I'll be damned if I let that happen."

Elspeth glanced at him. "Did you say something?"

"No, just thinking about the route ahead."

Her eyes narrowed and she nodded shortly, accepting his words at face value.

But the presentiment of danger remained.

# CHAPTER 13

*E*lspeth swiped the dust from her face, the heat of mid-morning stealing her energy. After four days on the road, she was gradually becoming accustomed to the dust and flies that seemed to gather in any place where there was a live creature or human. But the heat was energy sapping.

The jingle of harnesses caught her attention as Aeddan signaled they stop. Elspeth cupped one hand over her brow, searching the horizon to see what had suddenly caused his concern. There were trees and a shimmer, leading her to wonder if there was water ahead. Surely the horses would welcome a waterhole as much as she would.

One look at her husband's face, though, filled her with disquiet. Devil's Chaos snorted and pawed at the ground, as if sensing his master's concern.

"What's wrong, Aeddan?"

He stayed her with a sharp hand movement, and she waited as he gave an order. The men and their horses circled around her, and she sucked in a deep breath. Whatever concerned him, she surmised there was far more to it than ensuring she felt comfortable and safely escorted.

A rider appeared ahead and behind a palanquin was carried at a trot by men. It drew level and a hand appeared, curling imperiously, summoning Aeddan. He grimaced and dismounted, handing the reins to her before sauntering forward.

Whoever was within engaged in a sharp and short conversation with her husband. She noted that Aeddan reached within his coat and pulled out a packet of letters, sifted through them, and then handed one over. *Intriguing.* She filed the information away for discussion later.

Another quick, short conversation took place, too low for her to make it out, then Aeddan drew away with a low bow, receiving the letter that was pushed into his hands before the palanquin moved on. He stayed on the ground, watching for several minutes before heading back to the knot of riders. Remounting, he urged his mount forward.

"Who was that?"

"Merely a friend." His tone was dismissive, and for the first time she felt her ire rise. He was keeping secrets. She hoped they weren't dangerous ones.

"Aeddan..."

"Not now, Elspeth. We can discuss this later." His visage was grimmer, and though he'd adverted his gaze so she couldn't see his eyes, his jaw was more tightly chiseled than before.

He led them toward the river, this part of the journey being taken at a trot, until they reached the banks of the small body of water. "Come, dismount and let the men water the horses. This might be the last body of water we see until we reach Jessore."

She allowed him to take her hand and help her down. Then she stretched, working the kinks from her back and legs. "Aeddan, who was—"

"Later, Elspeth."

Anger writhed in her gut. Twice he'd cut her off without any explanation. If the heat and flies and her sore backside weren't enough, now she had this to contend with. If there were dangers ahead, surely she should know? After all, she was his wife and not some weakling miss.

"Why are you refusing to answer me, Aeddan? What's—"

He turned quickly, squeezing her hand. "Not now, Elspeth. It's not something I wish to discuss right at this point." In his eyes, she saw him pleading for her to accept his demand. As before, she quieted.

"Later. You'll explain later."

He bowed stiffly. "I have instructed the men to light a small fire and make tea. Then we eat before we continue. There is a tiny settlement ahead. One I'd like to make before the light fades."

"So we'll be staying..."

His face tightened further. "We'll encamp just within sight of the village."

She accepted his words, drank the proffered tea, and waited until they mounted once more, assessing what she knew of her husband.

He was a strong man, one who was open most of the time. Or at least gave that impression to those around him. She understood the majority of men would do anything to shelter their loved ones from harm. Maybe that's what this was? Perhaps she was jumping at shadows and had forgotten how to hand over control, and that was making her irritable?

They rode on, the heat taking its toll so that by the time they stopped for the night, she was exhausted. And she was sure her body was drained of all liquid.

Aeddan was there, helping her down to the ground, holding out a water skin. She drank deeply while the men went to work, setting up tents and lighting fires. He gripped a long, smooth stick in his hands, and she narrowed her eyes before dismissing it.

"Come." He led her to a bush not far away, rattling his stick, then gave a nod. He waited while she ducked behind it to relieve herself. As she emerged he held out the water, dribbling it over her outstretched fingers. "Wash your face. You'll feel better for it."

She did so silently, letting it splash her back to awareness. "Why, Aeddan?"

His lips tensed. "There's an outcropping I can see. Let us go sit and I'll explain all."

She let him lead her, the pale red of the dust kicking up beneath her feet to a mound of rocks. Elspeth made to sit down but he grabbed her shoulder. In the distance she could see the flickering lights of the township. The one they weren't staying in. She held her counsel on that subject.

"Wait."

She stilled, and he pushed and prodded, banged the rocks, and waited. A number of slow-moving bugs emerged, and he hissed. "Now you can sit."

"What was that all about?"

"Snakes and spiders out here can be dangerous. You need to be careful." The look on his face was tense, and she nodded.

"I will be."

He sighed then slumped down to the rocks beside her. "I have told you who I am, but not what."

Elspeth tensed at his words. "What do you mean? What? There are more secrets?"

"I'm a spy, Elspeth. I've been working with Lytton, trying to flush out the infiltrators in the Colonial Government. After your arrival, when I became aware that your father had been working with the government before his death, helping to send information back to England, as you know Lytton directed me to flush out those who'd try to control information for their own benefit. They were important dispatches—ones that needed to be sent covertly. However, it seems our enemies became aware at around the same time. The discussion earlier with the man on the Palanquin? It confirmed what we'd already suspected. That we have traitors in our ranks."

"Who are they?"

"Those who would sell out their countrymen? Spies in Government House. I was returning from overseeing a meeting between Russia and the Afghan Sher when I came aboard the *Zephyr*. It was more luck on my part. Lytton got word through other sources that they were going to try kidnapping you. Hold you prisoner until you to either refused to carry the information, or agreed to intercept it and copy it. Lytton needed you safe. And we need to find out who is leaking the sensitive information. Lytton plans to capture them while I have you far away—and this was the safest and most expedient way to ensure that."

Something inside her chest, the feeling of well-being that had grown in the last weeks, crumbled. Pain, excruciating pressure, replaced it.

He hadn't wanted her. It had all been a ruse. A part of his role as a spy.

"You..." She couldn't form the words. Her spine straightened, and she refused to let the tears form in her eyes. She wouldn't let him see how much his words speared her.

"Elspeth?" He leaned in, and she had to stop her instinctive reaction, the one that said *don't let him touch you.*

"You are a spy, for Lytton. I understand. Then I will do everything I can to help you." She couldn't let the emotions loose. Not yet. She needed to know it all. "The man you met on the road?"

"He's one of the lesser princes. The letter of introduction also requested safe haven if necessary and safe passage. He had information. I sent word back with one of the men I trusted."

She nodded wordlessly, deeply wounded by his words. "Fine."

For a moment she looked out, seeing the vista before her, the red-gold slashes that extended through the sky as night started to close in. The men moved about with efficiency, starting fires to cook over, the tents a dirty, dusty white against the ancient backdrop. Her hopes became ashes while they tended to their daily tasks. It was all so damned unfair.

"I find myself greatly fatigued. If you'll excuse me." She rose, calling on the innate dignity, cloaking herself in it.

"Elspeth, wait..."

"I..." The pressure bloomed again in her chest. She had to get away before the tears escaped from her burning eyes. "I should go change." Then she left him, striding across the sandy soil.

∼

*H*e knew the way she'd left him sitting there that he'd said something to upset her. But for the life of him, he couldn't work out what it was, exactly. She'd been stiff and formal in the way she'd left, and that had him confused.

Women had come and gone in his life, but he'd never really made attempts to understand them. No, it had always been about the pleasure—on both sides, of course. Now he was at a loss. His wife was no open book with easy to understand answers. For the first time, he wished he'd paid more attention in his younger years.

Aeddan searched the horizon, noting the streaks of red and gold fire stretching across the darkening vista. With the current political instability, you couldn't rely on anyone to act in any pre-determined manner. They could be safe here given the letter from Lytton that he'd presented to the prince, or they could come under attack at any time.

"God damn it!" He didn't have time to worry about his wife's behavior. He had their lives to be concerned with, he reminded himself ruthlessly, but that didn't soothe the restlessness or dissatisfaction.

Removing his hat, Aeddan brushed his hands through his hair as he thought over the information he'd gathered in Satkhira. Many he'd spoken to told of marauding gangs, and while he didn't discount the problems they might cause, he hoped there were no more organized mercenaries looking for them. He'd instructed the men under his command to prepare to leave Calcutta as early as he dared—well before dawn on the first day—but if anyone realized that they'd left as early as they did...

He narrowed his eyes, scanning the horizon once more, looking for any telltale signs of travelers or something more worrying, but it remained unblemished. The best they could hope for was clear day ahead. They'd been traveling slowly. Mainly walking the horses to allow them some rest, and they had a lot more baggage than usual.

If he'd been on his own, without Elspeth, he and his men would have traveled faster and longer each day, racing the horses against the clock. But she was a lady. Unused to long days in the saddle and the privations of this kind of travel. His mind told him he was underestimating her, but he ignored that.

He exhaled slowly, calculating in his head how to make their location as fortified as they could. Then he stood, stretching.

"I'll have to ask Elspeth what's wrong later," he muttered to himself.

Seeds of disquiet took root in his mind. What if there was more to her incomprehensible behavior? What if it was more than just tiredness and irritability? He shied away from those thoughts. That path led to the dreaded range of female issues that occurred monthly, from what his married friends had suggested in the past. Something he'd gladly laughed off as not of concern to him.

He strode toward the camp, checking his men's preparations for the coming night. They had set up a tent for himself and his wife as well as the one Grundy would share with the provisions. The rest of the men had fanned their bedrolls out in formation. He stopped, sharing a quick word with this man then another. He made his way calmly through the camp, checking to make sure everything was in order.

In the distance, several men hobbled the horses. The men would watch them through the night, checking for snakes and bugs and anything more sinister that might upset them. His own horse and Elspeth's would be kept apart. They were too valuable to risk. Besides which, Devil's Chaos seemed to settle better closer to him.

Grundy headed in his direction, his gaze flicking from side to side. "I've got your horse tethered to your tent, sir. The mistress's horse, silly thing it is, is tied to the other one. She's a tad too skittish to just hobble, according to the captain."

"That's to be expected." Aeddan frowned though at Grundy's words. She was perfect for such a trek, however, they hadn't had time to prepare her for nights in the open. He disliked having to act in haste, and this was a prime example of why.

He looked at Sana and Devil's Chaos, their heads in the feedbags as they chewed their rations. His own stomach growled, reminding him of the long hours since they'd last eaten. He turned on the heel of his boot and headed in the direction of the makeshift kitchen.

"*Sahib*, I have made a stew, but the meats..." His cook shrugged his thin shoulders.

For a moment Aeddan searched the coffee-colored man's face. It was as open as usual, and the tension in his muscles relaxed. "Yes. We will be able to purchase fresh at our next town."

They carried only the basics, in an attempt to travel as lightly as possible, but along the way there would be some overnight camps. Usually they didn't cause him too many headaches. This wasn't one of them though.

"*Sahib*, the meal will be ready soon, if you wish..." The man's words died away, and Aeddan gave a slight nod, making sure that the cook received the message. He would alert Elspeth.

The aroma of food wafted on the air as he lifted the flap of his own tent. The one he shared with his wife. Elspeth sat stiffly on the bedroll, tugging at her boots, the skin of her face red and tight.

"Let me help you."

She lifted her eyes as she clearly spoke. "No, thank you. I'm sure I can manage."

For a moment he searched her face, but she glanced away from him as the boot flew free, flying through the air to land at his feet. She humped and stood, reaching for the offending leather. He was there first, and scooped it up.

"Thank you." The words were waspish as she grabbed the shoe from his grasp then turned away. "I would like to change if you'd..."

"Elspeth..."

She didn't turn at his word though; her back remained his answer, and he wanted to sigh and ask what he'd done. *There'll be no answer here right now.* So instead, he kept his distance. "Dinner will be ready soon."

She nodded stiffly but didn't answer.

At a complete loss, he took one last look at the set of her back and shrugged. "I'll leave you alone then," he said before retreating through the tent flap.

# CHAPTER 14

*E*lspeth tossed and turned fitfully. Aeddan had joined her long after she'd retreated from the circle around which he and his men sat. She'd chosen the coward's route, pretending to sleep, though she was fairly sure he realized she was awake.

Watching the sway of the canvas through nearly closed lids, she remembered the looks he'd cast at her all night, but the turmoil in her mind was too great. Leaving their tent and sitting where he indicated, she'd avoided his gaze as much as she could. The anger and regret picked at her brain like one of the many birds of prey feeding on a dead carcass she'd seen along the trek. She'd barely made it through dinner, her stomach a roiling mass, before she excused herself.

In the cool of the night, she reflected on what she knew. He'd married her to keep her safe. That she could understand, but the subterfuge? The ruse of finding her attractive—making her think he craved her touch! The way he'd held her, and done a whole lot more each and every night! That went against everything she'd wanted in a husband. The fact he'd done it for the queen and the empire made no difference in her mind. He'd lied. He'd bedded her for his country but pretended he'd wanted only her.

Clasping her hand over her mouth, she swallowed the cry of pain that rose in her throat. She wouldn't let him know. *Couldn't.* All that was left was her pride, and she'd guard that zealously. Elspeth refused to consider that denying him the intimacy they'd shared every night since their marriage, even since they'd started this trek, was telling.

She had to face the truth. She had a husband whose body she ached to share, but he didn't feel the same. The fact was he engaged far more than just her body. He'd somehow stolen his way into her very soul.

Did she love him? That she couldn't answer, but she could truthfully say she desired him. Wanted him. Craved his touch.

She found herself replaying his words in her mind. *"I'm a spy."*

He'd married her because Lytton had commanded it, just as he'd commanded he keep her safe from harm. A hysterical thought bloomed: did that mean keeping her safe from the negative spiral of emotions? She shushed the thought.

Tears burned at the back of her eyes. In her mind, she'd built up her expectations. Of all the dreams she'd ruthlessly suppressed in the past, the ones that had been of a husband and children of her own were the most fragile, for they included the setting up of her own home with a man she could love and trust.

He'd smashed through the walls she'd erected over the years, those built of loneliness and the loss of hope, with his kisses and caresses. She'd been too damned gullible to realize it was all a practiced ruse.

Her pride ached at the massive blow it had taken. Had they also been part of his plan? Or did he feel some modicum of need for her? "Don't think that, Elspeth." But the whispered words didn't help.

"Elspeth?"

She gave an almost silent moan and held still, hoping he'd not push.

Outside she heard movement and the dull murmur of men

going about their duties. The soft, shuffling of feet while the pole in the middle of the tent shuddered as it had many times during the night. She knew Devil's Chaos was tied to the pole, where he felt most comfortable. Sana would be tethered to Grundy's tent. Aeddan had explained that she had not formed enough of a partnership with her rider to be safely hobbled with the other horses, and besides she was too valuable to be with them.

"*Sahib!*" The call went out, muffled from outside. It was enough to have him moving instantly.

Already Aeddan was sitting upright, reaching under the roll that served as a pillow. She too sat upright, her heart pounding madly.

Aeddan pressed a heavy pistol into her hands while hauling on a jacket. "Stay here. If anyone but me or Grundy enters, shoot them."

His face was grim, determined in the light of the tiny lantern which hung from the tent pole. It swayed back and forth in time with the shuddering movements from outside. Probably Devil's Chaos trying to escape the melee.

The flap of the tent closed behind him, well before she could break from the trance.

Her stomach roiled as she heard the sound of screaming horses, grunts, and thuds. Here and there silhouettes danced across the canvas of the tent, and she shuddered. There were men out there. Men determined to hurt them.

Why? Were these the men Aeddan worried about? Or were they simply opportunistic and starving?

Before her startled gaze, a hand thrust within, and though she trembled with fear, Elspeth held the pistol ready. Her hands shook. Aeddan had given instructions, and she would follow them through. The coffee-colored skin retreated, and she perspired heavily. It trickled down her back in a chilled trail as a sense of helplessness assailed her.

A last cry filled the air, and she waited with her fingers

cramped on the cold metal of the butt, only the wood bore any heat from her grasp. The sweat dried and chilled against her skin, making her shiver.

Once more the flap moved, and this time a pale hand preceded a body. Aeddan. She quivered and shook.

"You're fine?" His rasped words joined with the tight planes of his face as he glanced around.

Barely capable of speech, Elspeth nodded.

The exhalation was deep, and for an instant he closed his eyes. "Good. I have to go help clear away the mess. Stay here. Grundy is just outside if you need anything."

Then he was gone, and she was alone.

$\approx$

*A*eddan breathed deeply. Letting go of his storming emotions was so much harder than he'd anticipated. Pressure had built up in his muscles, and now that dissipated, lightness filling his mind. His limbs felt liquid, and his wits scattered like a dry wind as he tried to corral his emotions.

"She's okay. They didn't see her or get to her, Major."

Grundy laid a hand on his shoulder as Aeddan ran an unsteady palm over his whisker-covered chin. Aeddan stared forward, watching as his men cleaned away the signs of the brief yet bitter skirmish. A few of his men had sustained injuries, though thankfully, none of them serious enough to warrant slowing down their travel.

Two of the attackers were on the ground. Dead. His men would deal with the bodies once they had attended to their own needs.

"But she was in danger." The words hung there between him and his batman. There really wasn't anything else to say, was there? Bitterness swept through him. He'd brought her into danger, and now he regretted it.

"You protected her."

The well of anger swelled deep within his chest, a seething mass of emotions, all black and oily. "I should have sent her home."

"She wouldn't have gone. She's not that kind of woman, and you know it."

He closed his eyes, accepting the truth of Grundy's words. "No, she wouldn't." He couldn't do a damned thing about that. It did, however, clarify one thing in his mind. "Keep watch."

Then, leaving Grundy in the sparse light of the campfires, he spun on his heel, heading to the tent. He flicked the flap open and entered.

Elspeth remained where he had left her, huddled on the bed. Her face bone white, her hands clenched into one single fist in her lap. She watched him as he advanced.

"I shouldn't have left, but I had things to attend to."

She nodded without a word, and the lump in his throat grew. He should have addressed why she had refused to talk to him earlier. That silence had been bad enough, but now, facing his own mortality, and hers too, had propelled him forward. He needed to breach whatever gap was between them. She could have died with this nebulous chasm between them, and that was untenable.

"I'm sorry for earlier." She spoke hesitantly, and he frowned.

"Why?" The need to know why she'd withdrawn ate at him, as much as the knowledge that she was once more safe. *For now*, his mind added.

"Because it was childish of me." She lifted her chin, and it wobbled slightly. Her eyes shone in the half-light, glittering as one tiny diamond of water trembled on her eyelashes. It wavered then dropped, tracing its way down her porcelain skin.

That drip tore through his chest like a knife through butter. He couldn't contain himself as he reached out, cupping her cheek. He rubbed his thumb over her flesh, wiping away the tear, unable to ignore her pain.

"Why are you crying?"

"I don't know."

He smiled at the disgusted tone of her voice, but that melted away as she sniffled. "Earlier... You were angry."

She turned away, and it gutted him. He wanted to comfort her, but whatever it was, she didn't want the support he could offer.

"Tell me."

She shook her head, and not for the first time, he was conscious that she wore little more than a light shift, her hair tied back in a tight plait. Emotion welled again, lust and hunger combining as he caught sight of the berry-colored nipples through the fine white material. His body stirred to life.

"I can't..." She sighed, dashing at the tears with one ruthless tug.

"Tell me, Elspeth."

She hunched forward as if trying to stop the damage each quiet request made on her armor. "I don't want to."

"Please, Elspeth. I just want to help you, but I'm not sure how to do that without hurting you."

She snuffled harder, but this time she looked around at him, misery showing on her features. She moved, clutching at herself. "You... You already have." Her wet face glistened in the lamplight.

Confusion flooded him. "What? How?"

"You married me."

*What?*

Before he could speak, she continued. "I never expected to have a husband. It was so far from my expectations. Then you came along..." Her words trailed away. "You gave me hope, then took it away."

"How did you come to that conclusion?" He wanted to scoff at her words, but they were heartfelt, he could tell. The way she had hunched forward and wrapped her arms around her stomach while her eyes were wounded pools of misery. His heart clenched, and he shuddered. *What have I done to cause this?*

"You said... You stated that it was part of your role as a spy. That you married me under...under Lytton's command." Her husky voice tore at him.

"What? No! No, I didn't." But his mind stilled at her words.

"Yes, you did. Lytton told you to keep me safe, you said."

He shook his head, reaching out for her. She shied away, but he caught her against him. "No. No, Elspeth. That wasn't how it was."

Her tears soaked his jacket while the convulsive shudders told him of her deep pain. Regret pierced him.

"I married you because I wanted to. I desire you. Hunger for you. I've had to protect many others during my time as a spy. I never married any of the women. Please, believe me."

She raised her face to his. "But how can I believe that?"

"Because I've never felt this with anyone else." Then he kissed her.

# CHAPTER 15

$\mathcal{T}$he touch of Aeddan's lips on hers was magical. It stole her senses and filled her with the buzz of sensuality. For a moment Elspeth accepted the pleasure that spiked wildly, before the hurt caught her up. Worried her with its sharp teeth.

Spreading her fingers, she pushed against him. Away. Back. "No." She shuddered under the aftershocks.

His eyes, still passion-glazed, stared deep into hers, as if questioning her actions. "Elspeth..."

"This means nothing more than you hunger for my body." She couldn't—wouldn't—give in to that. The pain cut too deeply. Her knees shook under her fine shift, and she hoped he didn't notice the movement. "It's not enough. I won't let you hurt me. I can't." She panted, trying to hold her pain at bay.

"Elspeth... I..."

She shied away, hoping he wouldn't push. She wasn't sure she could manage if he prodded the tightly bound jumble of painful emotions. "Please, Aeddan..."

Even she wasn't exactly sure what she was asking for. All she knew was what they had couldn't sustain her. Wasn't enough to fill the emptiness in her soul.

"Elspeth, I didn't..." His hands descended on her shoulders, not letting her move out of his grip. She tugged, but his fingers dug deep. "Listen to me. I didn't marry you just because Lytton ordered me to." His voice shook as if he could barely restrain his emotions.

The slow thud of her chest began to speed up. "What?"

With careful moves, he turned her.

She didn't want to look. *What if this isn't real?* Oh, but how her heart yearned.

"Elspeth, I've never lied to you. I may have withheld some truths, which I deeply regret, but never have I lied. Lytton didn't force me to marry you."

She held her breath. "What... What does that mean then?" *What more could there be? What else hasn't he told me?*

He grimaced. "I really don't know." He whipped his head away, and she got the impression he was almost as lost as she was. But when he turned back to her, his face was calm. Composed. "I feel something for you. More than just this...this desire. I won't promise you anything I'm unsure of, because that would be cruel. I'll give you what I have though, including loyalty and monogamy. I promise to be honest with you, but I won't live a lie and pretend an emotion I don't feel."

She needed more, but all she could do for the moment was *settle*. How that burned her soul.

Elspeth gave a short nod. "Then that is where it must rest for the moment. Thank you for your honesty."

He grimaced again then raised a hand to cup her face. Instinctively, she covered his hand with her own, touching his skin briefly before she broke the contact. She drew away from him. Right now all she had left was her dignity and scraps of an emotion she refused to explore any deeper. She wouldn't jeopardize what small shred of herself she had left.

"Elspeth?"

She jerked back, startled. "We should sleep now." Her voice

was raspy, and he frowned. "We have another long day of travel ahead of us."

He nodded, and this time he broke the connection. "I need to check the men."

Without another word, Aeddan spun on his heels and was through the flap of the tent.

Elspeth lowered herself to the bed, settling under the light cover while listening to the chatter of the men outside. She strained, her eyes closed as she tried to pinpoint Aeddan's voice. Every now and again she thought she caught the sound, but it trailed away.

Pointless. Trying to sort out her feelings would no doubt confuse her further, she decided with a derisive huff. Pick at the wound and not only wouldn't it heal, it would probably grow some infection. Based on the current situation, she was sure it would be one likely to kill her—or at the very least, her sense of self.

He hadn't promised her anything except a future together and children. The future as *his* viscountess. Her stomach trembled as that fear rose. She didn't want that—had never sought a position so high. She just wanted the man she'd married. The major who'd awakened her senses and made her *feel*. Instead, what he now promised was so much more, and yet so little...from a man she barely knew. The knowledge he didn't love her hurt. It cut deeply—almost as much as the now erroneous realization that he'd only married her because he was ordered to do so.

*So where does that leave me?* With a groan, she opened her eyes, observed the stained canvas roof, and let her resolve firm.

"I'm no quitter." She couldn't say she loved him either, but there was a hit of a deep emotion, maybe a kind of yearning, she thought, growing inside her.

Perhaps with time she could entice something stronger from him. She'd heard the rumors of women in harems and how they used their wiles to tempt their husbands. For a moment her own thoughts shocked her before she began to assess it from all angles, as any business-minded woman would. It might work, *if* she had an opportunity to meet with some of those cloistered women and learn their secrets.

"Tomorrow. I can think about all these things tomorrow." She rolled over and closed her eyes, hoping sleep would come soon. Her senses, weary from the fright and emotional upheaval, began to drop away, and she welcomed the lure of sleep.

$\sim$

*A*eddan glanced sideways, noting the stiffness in Elspeth's profile as she rode beside him. She'd been quieter than at any time since their journey began. Since the attack days ago and their ensuing discussion, he couldn't seem to work out what she was thinking. In fact, he hadn't been able to connect with her at all. It was as if she wasn't truly even here.

She never complained during the long hours of riding, though he knew some days she ached. He could see it in the set of her lips and her stiff gait after hours in the saddle, yet she never voiced her discomfort. The nights were...perplexing.

He drew his horse closer. "Do you wish to stop?"

She looked at him, her face the mask she'd taken to wearing during the day. "Not right now, thank you."

By day she was the epitome of a well-educated English woman—remote and self-assured. By night, she was a *houri*. A woman who responded fully to his every embrace and touch, each caress richer than the last and each kiss a drug that drew him deeper into his addiction to her.

Elspeth had become a confusing enigma. In the space of this trek, she'd become the puzzle he didn't have time or the knowledge to piece together.

In the distance, he noted how the terrain changed. In the last few days, they'd ridden closer to the water's edge. The haze of shimmering heat gave way to a muddy brown, undulating ribbon. *Water.*

"We'll stop here and take a break," he ordered. "Then we can find our way to the town where we will gain transportation for ourselves and the horses."

His men dismounted, chatting. Elspeth clambered off the horse without waiting or seeking his assistance. He frowned.

"Elspeth..." Even as he slid down the side of his mount, she turned away, and his anger grew, his gut churning as she refused his help.

"I'd really like to freshen up a little." Without glancing in his direction, and grasping the reins in one gloved hand, she began patting at her split skirts, as if to remove every trace of dust from them.

"Elspeth..."

"Yes?" The imperious tone, stiff back, and glacial looks cut off any thoughts he had of rectifying the situation immediately.

"I'll arrange something." He sighed the words, realizing that at this point there wasn't any way to fix whatever vexed her. His men were watching eagerly, but he wasn't going to give them a scene. He stepped back and away. But by God, he'd find out what drove her and deal with it, at the first possible opportunity.

She inclined her head, and with a gentle tug, walked her mount forward, past him. He seethed. This wasn't how it was supposed to work. He didn't know how to chip away at the wall of ice she erected around herself each and every morning.

As she sashayed away he was left sweating. It was difficult to resist the urge to tug on the collar of the uniform he wore. Cupping a hand, Aeddan raised it to his brow and shadowed his eyes, watching her lead the horse to a small bowl of water.

"You've got your hands full there, sir. Let me take your mount." The man tugged the reins from his grip just as he caught sight of a plume of dust rising in the distance. He jerked forward, looking hard, but couldn't detect enough to be sure if it was friend or foe.

With great deliberation, he moved toward Elspeth, who was calmly rubbing the neck of her horse. It snickered as she spoke in a soothing tone.

"Move to the center of the camp, Elspeth."

She jumped. "You startled me!" Her tone was accusatory, but when he lifted a hand and pointed in the direction of the dust she followed it with her eyes. "Oh."

"Mount up!" Aeddan snarled.

The cry split the air, and she looked back at him, her face composed, though he was sure he detected a hint of uncertainty. With a swift nod she moved to the side, her hands gripping the pommel and cantle. He cupped his hands and boosted her back into the saddle. She settled with a hiss in the seat, legs astride. Then she wheeled Sana in the direction of the men.

Grundy was there, perched on his horse with the reins of Devil's Chaos thrust out toward him. He flung himself into the saddle and rode to wait beside Elspeth, who sat there adjusting her hat and gloves. Aeddan was more than a little startled, watching her careful ministrations.

"When meeting someone you are unsure of, it's always best to be prepared."

The urge to laugh bubbled. But it wasn't the time or place. Instead, he straightened his back and stared ahead. *Who is it?*

The riders advanced slowly in their direction, inexorably moving toward the knot of gathered soldiers clustered around Elspeth. The sounds, jingling harnesses and stamping hooves, came soon, and he could start to make out ten maybe fifteen men.

Devil's Chaos and Sana remained still while the other horses fussed, sidestepping and snickering.

"*Namaste.*" The man riding at the front of the party bowed over the horse's head, the palms of his hands pressed together.

Aeddan returned the greeting with a smile and waited.

"Sahib, you are a long way east of Bombay and Calcutta."
Dark eyes watched him as Aeddan's men stilled their prancing
mounts. The man spoke impeccable English though with a slight
accent.

"Indeed. We plan to proceed to Chandpur but seek a
conveyance capable of assisting us." He eyed the man specula-
tively, wondering who he was to be surrounded by black-
turbaned men, each with vicious curved blades at their side.

The man's surprise was quickly reined in. "Most travelers
organize boats in Barisal. However, I believe we can help you."

"Really?" He lifted an eyebrow, and the man laughed.

"Yes, but I feel your party is a trifle parched. Come, let us
take tea."

The suggestion threw Aeddan off his stride, and he stared at
the man who smiled warmly at Elspeth, and when she returned
the glance, he wanted to tear her away. A ripple of a dark
emotion, greasy and unwelcome, rose in his chest. He wanted to
roar with frustration but countered it with the knowledge he
hadn't yet been gifted with the man's name. He could be anyone,
though he had an air of easy command about him. Aeddan
watched as the man dismounted and smiled at his wife.

"Fair lady, allow me to assist you."

And damn, if she didn't just let him do that.

Aeddan seethed.

～

*S*he knew Aeddan was angry. It was apparent in the set
of his shoulders, and the terse answers and fulminating
glances he sent in her direction. She quaked a little, knowing how
furious he must be, but some seed of devilry had planted itself
deep, so she accepted the man's assistance and arm. She sat down
on the jeweled cushions his men produced and sheltered
beneath the hastily erected tent.

As their host chatted she nodded and accepted a cup of fragrant tea. She knew Aeddan watched her every action. She took her time; each sip allowed her a chance to study her husband from below her dipped eyelashes.

He was an impressive man, but given to secrets, she'd come to understand. Whether they were resultant from his role as a spy or from his innate training since childhood, she still had to determine. But there were times when his body telegraphed his current state of mind. This was one of them. Aeddan sat upright and stiff, and she wanted to sigh her frustration at his cold demeanor.

"So, you wish to travel the Sendha River and cross the Meghna?"

"Yes. Myself, my *wife*, and our entourage are traveling to Maijdee. We hope to meet with silk weavers."

The man opposite smiled. "Ah, yes. Their work is quite exquisite. But tell me, what does a man like you, obviously well connected and educated, want with the weavers?"

The man displayed the grin of a crocodile, Elspeth thought privately. All teeth and more, it hinted at a hidden danger. She repressed a shiver at the ridiculous thought.

"I am investigating a business arrangement." Aeddan's tone became hard and cold. "I'm sure you understand."

"Indeed, *sahib*." The man inclined his head. "Come then, if your good wife is done, let us ride to the river. I have men who will secure you a boat to carry yourselves and your horses safely to the other side."

"That is most gracious of you."

Aeddan relaxed a little, and she wondered why he now felt that it was safer. She felt more confused than ever before. They still didn't know the man's name or what he wanted. She stole a glance at Aeddan, but he wasn't looking at her.

"Aeddan..." She kept her voice low, but he shook his head, no doubt to hush her, and she frowned.

He knew India better than she did, so she acceded to his unspoken request, took his proffered hand, and rose. At the edge of the tent, Grundy waited, holding the reins of Sana and Devil's Chaos.

Sana snickered as Elspeth touched her long face. "Hello, my lovely."

"What a beautiful mount you have there, *memsahib*. She is an Arab, is she not?"

The man startled her. Now he was standing just behind her shoulder, and she raised a hand to her chest, as if to still her rapid heartbeat. "Indeed, she is. My husband purchased her for me before we left Calcutta."

The man smiled benignly. "Let me offer you assistance." He gestured to the saddle.

"I thank you for offering your help to my wife, however I will help her into the saddle."

Aeddan's voice was brusque, and she breathed deeply, hoping to wash off the aggravation that once again rose. Without a word, she placed her foot into the cradle of his hands, and he boosted her up then handed her the reins.

The men swung atop their mounts, and with a quick command, the Indian turned his horse to the water with Aeddan following. She glanced behind, seeing the way the men snapped to attention before she followed her husband as they fell into formation behind the two of them.

# CHAPTER 16

*A*eddan barely held onto his temper. He knew Elspeth was trying to be the wife he wanted by making few demands on him during the day, but in the instant when the man made to touch her, his possessive nature had risen. It nearly smothered him in the intensity, and it left him both confounded and angry.

What was it about Elspeth that made him need to protect her? To keep her for himself?

The road ahead changed from sparsely covered ground to lush and green. Verdant. Their pace slowed as the ground became softer. The clank of the decorations worn by the horses fought with the sounds of migratory birds and the rustle of greenery as they made their way through the long grasses.

"Wait, *sahib*." Finally the man—Aeddan knew he was high caste—held up a hand. He carefully dismounted and handed his reins over. The horse stepped and whinnied fretfully. "Wait here while I converse with these men."

Just beyond the water's edge was a group of small boats, the men wearing little more than loincloths as they worked on their nets. The Indian, one who Aeddan suspected was a prince, carefully picked his way down before conversing. The men spoke to him with reverential tones while Aeddan watched. One man nodded profusely and picked up his nets before turning his boat away, but Aeddan remained still as the Indian made his way back toward him.

"He has knowledge of others with boats that can navigate down to the Meghna. They will meet you a little further north of here as the tide turns. There you will find a dock. It isn't a difficult ride, but one where we might pass tigers. We will ride with you and perhaps find ourselves some live game."

Aeddan had never participated in a tiger hunt, finding it barbaric, but he understood that it was a cultural pastime. "Indeed, and we welcome the company."

"Then perhaps you might join us?" The question was innocent but Aeddan had to think fast to avoid any insult.

"You honor me, but we cannot stop, for our mission requires us to be hasty in our travel." He gave a slight bow and hoped it would be accepted in the manner it was offered.

"Mission, *sahib*?"

Aeddan wanted to swear. His slip could potentially jeopardize their plan. "Err, yes. My wife and her sister traveled from England on a mission to find out more about their suppliers." His heart thudded slowly in his chest as the Indian smiled.

"Really? Your wife?" He cast an assessing glance at Elspeth, but she gave the impression of being unaware. Aeddan gritted his teeth.

"She is a woman of many talents. All of them dear to me." He hoped the implication was clear—he kept what was his, and Elspeth was one of them.

"Yes, *sahib*. Well, we have several hours of traveling ahead of us. Come, let us ride." The Indian remounted then wheeled his horse around and it jumped forward.

⁓

hey'd arrived some time earlier, and now Elspeth sat on a blanket, holding Sana's reins. The noonday heat was enervating, but she had to be patient. If she'd learned anything since her arrival in India, it was that nothing was quick.

She waited while Aeddan spoke with several Indian men, including their host. Shading her eye with a cupped hand, she glanced at the water. It was a muddy ribbon that undulated through the land. A wooden boat had pulled up to the gangway, sitting high in the water. It didn't really look terribly watertight, and she shuddered at the thought of crossing the deep, crocodile-infested river.

India, it seemed, was the ultimate land of deception. Nothing was quite as it seemed. She flicked away the flies that swarmed around with a lazy hand and waited while the negotiations continued.

"Excellent. We'll settle the balance on arrival." Her husband rose from the blanket where he'd been conducting business and handed over a pouch containing some sum of money. His gaze shifted in her direction, and a thrill of pleasure zinged through her, until his gaze slid over her shoulder.

Looking at him confused her. She wasn't rightly sure why, just that it did. On one hand, she was compelled to be with him, open to him intimately as much as she craved, yet she also had to protect the essence of herself.

The prince, for she was sure that was his title, moved closer. "*Memsahib*, if you will forgive me, my wife is nearby and has sought an audience with you. Would you permit this?"

Elspeth blinked. "Oh yes, of course."

"Then I shall send for her. Remain where you are, if you will."

He turned, spoke sternly to one of the men, and they scurried away. The heat of the sun bore down on her. Grundy brought her a pannikin of tea, which she was grateful for, and some fruit, before a cache of riders approached.

As the dust flew up, Aeddan drew close. "What's happening?"

She gestured toward the rising plume. "I believe it's the wife coming to pay me a visit." His stare had her shrugging. "She asked for a meeting, and I said yes."

Once more, the prince wandered toward where she sat, with Aeddan standing over her. "*Sahib, memsahib,* if you will permit me to introduce my wife, Amber. She was rescued as a child from slavers, and my father felt that she would be an excellent wife for me."

The wife was petite and dark-haired, curved in all the right places though swathed in a saree of the most wondrous turquoise. The jewel crusting had Elspeth itching to reach out and touch.

"It is my honor and pleasure, *sahib, memsahib.*" She placed her hands together and whispered, "*Namaste,*" and Elspeth returned the greeting.

"What a beautiful saree, Princess Amber."

The prince harrumphed, "Amber is best here, *memsahib.*"

"Of course."

The men drifted away, allowing the women to sit together. "You travel with your husband. Is that not unusual, and in such dress?"

Elspeth laughed. "I guess so, but my husband is escorting me to meet with the weavers who stock my ships with silks. But looking at your saree, I wonder if it wouldn't be wiser to meet with your weavers."

The woman laughed, a tinkle. "You go to Lakshmipur then? There are weavers of exceptional skill there. Will you return this way?"

With a shrug, Elspeth explained, "I'm not quite sure. My husband has the route organized."

"If you do, *memsahib*, it would be my pleasure to host you in the harem."

Elspeth stiffened, but the woman touched her hand.

"No, you misunderstand me. My husband has taken no other wife, for he is Christian and educated in the European fashion. I mean only to extend a welcome to your husband and yourself."

The words touched Elspeth. "Then I thank you and will discuss this with my husband. Yours indicated you were taken by—"

"I traveled with my family when I was young. Bandits killed my parents and their guard. Then they took me to the marketplace. It was there the princess found me and took me to be her daughter and friend to her son. Rajhendra was not much older than me, and his mother, the Princess Rani, had lost all her other children. They had already become Christians, so when the princess heard of me, they sent for the slaver. Brought me into their home and raised me as a suitable wife for him. On his return from Oxford, we were wed."

There was a wealth of emotion in the words, and Elspeth felt the urge to hug the woman.

Instead, she reached out and patted her hand. "Do you remember your family?"

The woman blinked. "Only a little. Rajhendra found my family and made contact, but they didn't want to know. So, the princess and prince became my family and cared for me. Now I'm proudly Rajhendra's wife. But you? My husband wrote that you were a woman of trade? Is that not unusual?"

Elspeth laughed. "A little, yes."

She'd just settled in to talk about her life when Aeddan caught her eye and the prince beckoned his wife. As she moved to join her husband, the princess whirled to face her. "Please, if you can, come visit with me on your journey home."

The hunger she heard in the woman's tone pushed her to accept. "I will."

Aeddan strode over, followed by Grundy. Aeddan helped her up after handing Sana's reins to Grundy. "You were deep in conversation."

"We have been asked to visit at the harem of ah..."

"Indeed?" Aeddan's eyebrows shot up. "Then you are privileged."

# CHAPTER 17

*I*t took a week for them to arrive at their destination in Maijdee. Torrential rain, muddy roads, and difficult conditions had slowed them down. The small village appeared to be in reasonable condition, and the housing Aeddan had procured for them was adequate, though not palatial.

The night of their arrival, they were exhausted and filthy, along with soaked to the skin as a cloudburst had opened half a mile from their destination. Grundy had taken care of Sana and Devil's Chaos, and all Elspeth could wish for was a warm bath, some food, and sleep.

"Come up. The landlord assures me the rooms are ready."

Aeddan ushered her into the apartment, deep furrows of white bracketing his mouth and eyes as she cradled her arm, deeply bruised from a fall the day before when a snarling dog had spooked Sana.

"Once Grundy has the horses settled he and the cook will begin preparing a meal. I've asked for water to be drawn for you. If you'll excuse me for a moment, I'll return to assist you."

Aeddan retreated from the room leaving her alone. He didn't

shut the door, fully as they'd filled the entire hotel with their men and Aeddan had set guards on the stairs ensuring their privacy.

"Thank you." She muttered to herself as she settled onto the bed, frustrated and keen to help herself, although well aware he'd pulled out a chair for her to sit in. Elspeth lifted one leg then the other, attempting to divest herself of the boots. They didn't budge, and her arm hampered her attempts.

Elspeth sighed and slumped back on the mattress. This journey had been more arduous than she'd expected or could have imagined. At least Isabelle wasn't there. Given her frailty, it would certainly have been too much.

The sound of feet was followed Aeddan's mutter of "let me help you." He carefully stripped the leather shoes from her feet, and she sighed with relief, wiggling her toes a little.

Her eyes fluttered closed as she inhaled deeply, thankful that for the first time in weeks, she'd have a bed to sleep in. Her body felt pummeled and abused by the privations of weeks of sleeping in tents, no matter how good the pallet Grundy had devised.

"I think you should rest tomorrow." Aeddan settled onto the mattress beside her.

"No. I'm here to meet with the weavers, and my man here locally will be expecting me." She cracked open an eyelid and stared at him. "Forster Shipping is reliable and on time. I'm not going to compromise that because I've been traveling."

He opened his mouth to respond, but the knock on the door stopped the words—whatever they may have been.

"Come in."

She sat up and swung her legs to the side of the bed as two young women dragged in pails of steaming water. "For bathing, *memsahib*."

Aeddan also rose, moved to the far wall, and watched as they continued their task in silence.

She waited until the women finished their work then left.

Aeddan rested against the jamb, and she allowed her gaze to roam over him. "Sir, are you waiting for something?"

His eyes gleamed. "Perhaps."

Elspeth considered his answer, at a loss to understand what he might possibly require—given she was sore and more than just mentally exhausted. "Uh, perhaps we could discuss this later?" she suggested, her need to wash the mud and muck from her body reaching epic proportions.

"In Calcutta you'd have a lady's maid to attend to your needs."

Understanding flashed, and while her body heated, she wasn't sure that his advances would be welcome. "Well, I'm sure tomorrow—"

Aeddan's gaze clouded. "Elspeth—"

"I just want to bathe, Aeddan." She did, that was true. If she were totally honest with herself, she would also accept that the coolness that had grown between them wasn't encouraging, and she didn't have a clue how to bridge it.

"Damn it, Elspeth, don't be hard-headed." He jerked away from the wall and stomped over to her. "I'm not going to attack you. Let me help you with your clothes, then I'll leave you in peace."

Pinpricks of stinging emotion battered her senses. She'd read him wrong, and he didn't want her. *Damn you, Lord Lytton!* The mess of her life she could lay wholly and solely at his door. Now her husband was more than happy to act the lady's maid and leave her to it.

He started unfastening and sliding the cloth from her body, the careful touch setting off sparks of excitement. Ones that would be unfulfilled.

With a deep breath, she stepped away from him. "I'll be fine, husband. If you'll excuse me?" Gathering the tattered threads of her dignity, she shuffled to the bathing room and shut the door.

On a sigh, she dropped her grimy shirt to the floor. The light corset and chemise puddled with the trousers and pantaloons he'd somehow arranged before they'd begun the journey. Bare, except for the stockings on her feet, she gazed upon herself in the mirror.

Her hands slid over her breasts, the bounty heavy and tipped with pink nipples. He'd sucked at them, like a babe would, and declared them beautiful.

She slid her hands down her body and over her belly, toward the dark red thatch of hair that hid what she now knew as a place of sexual delight. He'd spread her legs, held them open, and feasted upon her. Memories of the sensual actions heated her blood.

A tiny tear dripped down her face.

He hadn't wanted her these last few days. Had slept beside her and yet not once reached for her. She'd hoped that side of their marriage would be repaired once they'd settled here, only to be dashed again.

Tearing her gaze away from her reflection, Elspeth stumbled toward the small hip bath, stripped off the stockings, and slid gratefully within the water.

~

*A*eddan gazed at the heavy wood that separated him from his wife, his hands bunched into fists as he attempted to consider what he'd said or done that had forced them so far from the happy couple they'd begun this journey as. She'd banished him and on that thought he headed down stairs, toward the common eating area, needing some space to consider what had changed Elspeth.

A rap on the main door splintered his concentration, and when Grundy called out, he opened it to admit his man. Grundy had been with him for over ten years. For all that, he didn't even know if Alfred Grundy had a wife or sweetheart somewhere.

He waited until Grundy settled a pile of food in front of himself and lowered into a chair.

"You're not married, are you, Grundy?"

The man stopped abruptly. "Married? Me, Major? No. Tried it once, and it didn't stick."

Surprise sparked. "You were married?"

"Nah. Courting. She were a vicar's daughter and the prettiest thing you ever saw. Thought she was the one. Went to see her father, and she'd been courting another at the same time. I were too slow, and he snapped her up. Left Putney that day, ain't never been back since." Grundy started to eat without glancing at Aeddan. "Your missus ain't like that, sir, begging your pardon. She's a looker and all, but she's straight, like a bullet."

Aeddan waited for the man, sure there would be more said. Grundy finished his food.

"She's not like the other ladies though. Jacinthe told me she never expected to wed 'cause she's too old. Her and her sister came here looking to make a difference after her younger sister married."

The words Grundy spoke made no sense. No expectation? She was gorgeous, courageous, and caring. How could she see herself as on the shelf?

It was true that most men of his station married pretty, young things they'd met at balls and routs without two pennies worth of brains to spare, but the few young women he'd met had been downright vacuous. He'd not followed any generally accepted conventions, instead choosing to forge his own path before settling down to his family's estates.

He left Grundy in the common room and headed up the stairs, where he waited, listening for sounds from within the bathing chamber. There was only silence, and he frowned. Three steps had him at the doorway. He knocked. Knocked again.

Silence.

His gut churned, and he turned the knob, peered within.

Elspeth slept, slumped in the bath, her hair a tumbled and damp mass, while the sight of her breasts, pink-tipped and delicious, made his groin ache. The arousal was damped through by the bruising he caught sight of. Angry red marred the perfect skin of her left arm, from elbow almost to shoulder.

He'd pushed her too hard to make it here. In that moment it didn't matter that he'd been concerned that they'd be waylaid. He'd wanted her safe so they'd marched on.

Aeddan reached down, and she stirred as he lifted her.

"Wha..." she said, her voice slurred.

He gathered her close, seeking the bath towel to wrap around her before carrying her to the bed where he laid her down.

"Aeddan. I fell asleep." Her voice was thick.

"You did, Elspeth. Come, dress and eat some supper. Then you should rest."

While Elspeth obeyed in silence he castigated himself again. He watched to ensure she had settled into the chair then perched on the side of the bed beside her. They ate in silence, and the intimacy wound itself into the air, spicy scents and long moments of quiet interspersed here and there by gay chatter from outside the building.

When they'd finished, he tugged her close, while the thud of her heart settled and slowed. She didn't argue when, wordlessly, he lifted the covers and she slid within. He adjusted the net curtain over the bed, and she rolled to her side, her eyes closed.

Her breathing evened out, and Aeddan strode to the shuttered window, tugged at the wood, and peered out.

*Quiet.*

He could rest. He should sleep. Glancing at his wife who lay peacefully in the bed, he vacillated. She would welcome him, his advances. The passion between them was hot, and yet, his emotions were tangled. He wanted more than he had, but his mind refused to settle on love as the dominant mental state.

Was it right? Had he done the right thing? Too many questions formed in his mind without answers. He tugged the shutters closed. There'd be no answers tonight.

He shrugged out of his clothes and retreated to the bathing area.

~

*E*lspeth stretched, a feeling of comfort and well-being flooding her body as she sat up in the bed. It wasn't home. It wasn't the *Zephyr*, and she wasn't at North Point.

Memories crowded; entering the town last night, her weariness, bathing. "I fell asleep."

The room echoed, and she looked around and down. Her night-rail was in place. The bed beside her was untouched, and the sting of tears battered at her as did the sense of loneliness.

She flung the covers aside and rose, refusing to allow herself to fall into despair. If her marriage was a sham, then so be it. She'd wanted the passion and had gotten it.

She'd make the best of the situation, and perhaps on her return, she might find a suitable partner for Isabelle. Someone who would make her sister happy.

Snatching off her clothes and climbing into the fresh shirt and pants took little time. Elspeth crossed the room and tugged on the door.

Outside sat a guard, rumpled and obviously weary. "Begging your pardon, Mrs. Fitzsimmons, but the major stepped out earlier to make arrangements. He asked that you remain in the room."

Elspeth's lips tightened. "Thank you, Hitchens, but I need to organize my business. If there's another guard? I have an appointment with my man this morning, and I won't be late."

The guard blinked, clearly unsure what to do. "Uh, ma'am, if I allow you to do that, he'll have my head. I'll send for the major though."

She gave him the glare most at home would recognize as her do-it-now look and watched as he scurried off. Retreating back to the room wasn't satisfactory, but at least she'd begun to reassert the Elspeth she had always been. Settling herself on the bed, she prepared to wait.

When the door swung open several minutes later, she looked up and her husband entered the room, a scowl on his face. "My dear, this is not Falmouth where one can simply saunter down the street."

"Of course not. But I have a shipping line to run, weavers to meet, and orders to place. Too many people rely on me for me to become a shrinking violet. So husband, if you wish to attend me, do so, otherwise find me someone you trust."

"Elspeth—"

"No, Aeddan. I have people relying on me to complete my tasks." She curled her hands into fists. "Don't ask me to change, as I haven't asked you to."

He exhaled, shoulders slumping. "Take Grundy. I have a meeting with the head of the local regiment."

"Thank you. Is Grundy ready now?"

Aeddan gave a bark of laughter. "I forgot how strong-willed you can be, Elspeth." His grin melted away. "Yes. Take a guardsman with you too though, please."

"Of course." She went to the door, her hand settling on the knob, then looked back. "Your meeting...will it be long?"

"I don't know. It all depends on what he's heard or seen."

He'd evaded answering fully, the way his gaze slid over her shoulder, but she wouldn't push him to explain further. She knew her role as wife to a spy and had her own tasks to accomplish.

Without another word, she hurried into the hallway.

# CHAPTER 18

*S*ana sidestepped as they retreated from the Meghna River, discomforted by the rough journey on the barge back to this side of the river. Elspeth carefully rubbed her neck and spoke soothingly to the fractious mount in the hopes that she'd settle soon.

They'd spent a week in Maijdee while Elspeth had arranged her orders, met with the weavers, and inspected the factory, which turned out to be a cleared section of ground. Elspeth wasn't sure what she'd expected. Maybe some kind of building with large machines, not the rows of loinclothed men. Her mind was still overwhelmed by her experiences in India.

She turned in the direction she remembered they'd come when Aeddan grabbed her reins. "We're heading this way."

"What?" Surprise colored her tone.

"You have a meeting." He spoke quietly to her, and his words filled her with pleasure.

"Amber?"

"Yes."

The party formed up, with Elspeth riding next to Aeddan, Grundy a little ahead of them along with several men, and the others behind them. The terrain once more stable and dry, Sana settled into a comfortable walk.

"We cannot stay more than tonight."

Elspeth bit her lip at Aeddan's careful tone—the one he'd taken to using with her. It hurt, but she refused to allow the chasm between them to wound her anymore. If he was unable to be honest with her, that was his choice, but she wouldn't grant him any more chances to cut her with his omissions that were more like untruths.

One hour passed, the heat of the sun beating down on the party, before they spied a building before them. It wasn't as ornate as some of the palaces they'd passed. The gray stone building looked to only have two storeys, but Elspeth knew it was likely much bigger on the inside than her view could take in, hidden as it was beneath large, established trees.

As they drew closer, a company of soldiers appeared. Aeddan indicated they should stop while he conversed with those waiting for them. Grundy moved closer to Elspeth, and she waited until Aeddan returned.

"We're to follow this man. He will escort us to the entrance where we will be met by His Excellency."

Excitement quivered through Elspeth. She'd been looking forward to meeting with Amber again, the Caucasian woman who'd married this Indian Prince.

At the entrance, they dismounted and filed up the steps, Grundy just behind Elspeth while Aeddan took the front. Once the formalities of greeting passed, Elspeth was ushered to the women's quarters where Amber reclined on a bed set up beside a pond.

The woman looked up and smiled. She rose gracefully and advanced, her hands outstretched. "You came." Amber's smile was filled with delight. "You must come and rest after such a difficult journey. Did you find the weavers you sought?"

Elspeth found herself pulled along and made to sit beside the princess. "I did, Your Excellency."

"No! We will be friends, Mrs. Fitzsimmons. I shall call you Elspeth, and you shall call me Amber. I have so few people I can talk to as equals." Amber clapped her hands, and a woman into her third decade entered the room with a deep bow. "Bring us tea, then we are not to be disturbed."

The woman scurried away without a sound, and Elspeth shook her head. This was so alien from every other experience she'd had. The lush surroundings, white walls shuttered with elaborate designs at the high windows. The tiles and deep, plush seats grouped around the pond. Paintings of turquoise and gold on the wall, some of them quite erotic in nature. The scent of flowers and incense filled her senses. She'd hoped to visit a harem and was fairly sure that's where she now was.

"His Excellency informed me that there was talk of riders. I had hoped it was your party returning and you'd remember your promise." They talked as the tea arrived and was poured, then Amber spoke quietly. "You seem lost, my friend. Is there something you wish to discuss?"

Elspeth bit her lip, unsure who to trust, but needing advice from another married woman. Her innate sense of character told her Amber could be trusted.

"I don't know. I mean, I have no family, and I'm unsure..." Elspeth glanced away. "My husband married me because he was instructed to." The words came out strangled and with a miserable tone.

"Oh. A marriage of convenience. I see. My husband spoke of them when he returned to India. That many have no passion or fire, the men are miserable and turn to the comforts of other women—"

"No! It's not like that. There's plenty of...*excitement*. Well, before. But we argued and..." Heat flushed her face, and she ducked her head.

Amber sighed loudly. "You wish to engage your husband fully and don't know how?"

Elspeth scrubbed her hands over her eyes, which remained averted. "That's not exactly it. He's not unfaithful. He's caring and strong. But he doesn't love me. When we wed I believed that he wanted me, but it seems that was a lie." Saying the words embarrassed Elspeth deeply, but she needed help.

The woman beside her patted her hand. "If your husband does not want you, then I'll become a monkey."

Elspeth sat up at her words, her wide eyes now focused on Amber.

"My dear, he watches you like an eagle does its favored meal. There is heat and hunger between you, and it's obvious to a casual observer." Amber leaned closer. "He desires you, Elspeth. Hungers for you. You must merely allow the capture."

Elspeth stilled. Considered Amber's words. "He was very clear in his words to me. And I don't..." Standing, Elspeth moved to the fishpond and gazed into its depths.

"Men are illogical creatures." The jingle of Amber's jewelry echoed in the chamber as she moved her arm. "They say one thing but mean another, and the words they use are deceptive."

Elspeth whirled back to remonstrate, but Amber raised her hand, stopping her.

"They are not untruthful, but they're not expected or encouraged to discuss emotions. Perhaps the words he chose did not explain fully the emotion he attempted to convey?"

"I'll need to think about that." The words offered new insight, and Elspeth felt that she should investigate it fully.

Meanwhile, a light repast was delivered, redolent with figs and dates. Wine was served from a jug, and Elspeth enjoyed the time until Amber rose. "I will show you to your chamber. Your husband will be next door."

Together, the two women made their way down a short corridor. When Amber opened the door, it was to a room that oozed luxury and passion. It was decorated in purples and gold, the ceiling high and intricately carved and painted. Deep cushions scattered across the bed and low seats reinforced her summation that this room was meant for pleasure.

When Amber withdrew, Elspeth inhaled deeply, the incense and floral tributes in this chamber as luscious as those in the audience room they'd vacated.

She roamed the guest room, inspecting everything until her eyes settled on a book. The cover was ornately covered with jewels, and Elspeth opened it. Her gaze settling on the vision before her, a surprised "oh" filled the air.

The image depicted was a man and a woman...in an intimate pose.

With a trembling finger, Elspeth turned the page. Another intimate scene greeted her.

The door behind her opened, and she whirled, her cheeks flaming with heat as Aeddan looked at her.

"Elspeth? Is everything fine?"

Her fingers shook, and she touched her mouth. "Oh, yes."

He came closer, and her memory seized on the images she'd seen, interposing it with herself and Aeddan. Thoughts and hungers rose, swirled, and threatened to drown her in a sensual sea. The closer he came, the more her breathing became erratic. When he reached her, one hand extended, the air around them turned heavy.

"I..."

"Elspeth?"

"Aeddan. There's this book. It's..." She gulped the words, unsure of his reaction.

"Book?"

She whirled and pointed. "The book."

When she turned back his grin turned wolfish. "Ah, the *Kama Sutra*. I've heard of it. Saw one at a distance once. Not this particular one of course."

"You've heard of it? There's more than one?" Intrigue rose. When would he have seen that, and how did he know of such volumes?

"These books are legendary here in India. Each is individual in style or binding, yet they contain the same teachings. Come, show me."

*Oh God!* He was her husband, surely it wasn't right to share this intimacy with him! Temptation warred with embarrassment though, and she choked out, "But it's... They're... They're naked! Or only semi-clothed, Aeddan!"

"I had heard that before. Come, let us sit and investigate it."

She staggered to the bed as he reached for the book then followed her to settle on the deep coverlet. He opened the book, and as before, her body betrayed itself, heating and firming.

"Do you know any of the terms they refer to the body with?" His voice carried a dark, warm tone, one that washed over her and promised pleasures.

"I... No."

"The woman has the yoni, and the man the lingam. She is the sacred temple, and he is the jade stick. The jade stick yearns to enter the yoni. To know pleasure." Silence stretched as they studied the artwork, then he turned the page, uncovering another scene. "The woman has the pearl, a precious jewel of pleasure, Elspeth."

"Oh..."

He turned the page again, and another image appeared. A couple on a bed, and her breath caught. Fluttery sensations took wing in her belly as her mouth dried. "Is that... Surely no one could do that?"

He laughed, and the sound reverberated through her. "It's possible. But perhaps you would try something different? Simply breathe, my love. Inhale deeply and release the air in your lungs. Grant me your breath."

She did as he commanded, feeling silly. What he asked was easy. When Aeddan demanded she do it again, Elspeth did.

"Keep doing it. Breathe deep through your lips."

She did.

"Feel it all the way through your body. Down to here." He gently touched her stomach. "Feel it inside you. Concentrate on the sensations." His hand shifted, covering her abdomen and sliding further. "Here too." He cupped her between her legs, and she felt the heat, the melting sensation that betrayed her hunger to him. "Concentrate on the way you sit, the tingle of your body."

Doing so, awareness bloomed, and as she squirmed, it enticed her further into the web of desire.

"Let me love you, Elspeth. Let me adore you." He drugged her with words, the carnality of his voice chipping away at her thoughts.

"Yes," she breathed. Her mind whirled madly, reminding her that it seemed an eternity since he'd last touched her like this.

"Good. Keep breathing, my beauty. Concentrate, with your eyes closed, on your body. Don't let anything outside this room interrupt."

When Aeddan reached for the closure of her gown, she let him, felt each and every button, the release of her chemise and corset until she sat on the bed naked from the waist up while he whispered of her beauty. It amazed her that without sight the world melted away until there was just the two of them. This room. The scent and touches.

"Your breasts are firm, and the tips pink like luscious berries. Perfect for me. I love to feast on them, to place my mouth on you and suckle." Light touches reinforced his words, and she bowed into them.

"Aeddan?"

"Relax, my love." His hands rested lightly on her shoulders, then he started moving, tiny circles of pleasure. Each move more careful than the last.

"Aeddan, will you let me touch you?"

"Not tonight, my sweet. Tonight I will pleasure you. Only you."

Elspeth surrendered to the pleasure he heaped on her. Every slide of his hand heightened her senses, as his fingertips glanced her rib cage, then slid further south, dipping into her navel.

"Your belly is soft and rounded. Womanly. Just right for me." He kissed and laved the skin he'd uncovered, and she moved, lying beneath him.

With gentle hands, he disrobed her, until she lay bare. His hand hovered over her mound, then touched. Extending his finger, he slid his hand along her labia in a gentle exploration.

"I want to kiss you, my sweet. Will you let me?" The glance of exhaled breath teased her skin.

"Please, Aeddan."

The whisper of his breath left her knees quivering as he bent and replaced the touch of his finger with that of his mouth.

"*Ohhh...*" She gripped the coverlet, fingers digging deeply and twisting the linen as pleasure exploded in her belly.

"Keep breathing."

Without thought, she opened for him, needing the touch desperately, as her body quickened. Emboldened by his actions, she arched up, her eyes snapping open. "I want you, Aeddan."

He glanced up, their gazes meeting. *Melding.* She loved the way he looked in the throes of passion, face a study of harsh lines and somnolent eyes.

"Please, Aeddan. Come to me," she crooned.

He slipped off his coat. "Tell me what you want, Elspeth. Give me your words."

"I want you. I need to feel you, the way you slide inside me. How you touch my breasts. I need to feel your skin brush against mine." Girlish embarrassment held no place here, in this chamber with a lover who lavished her with such attention.

His shirt disappeared, then he reached for his pants and

shucked them. "I want you. I want all of you. I love being inside you. You complete me."

Clothes abandoned, he crawled back to her, miles of sun-tanned skin, the rasp of his cock against her inner leg ratcheting her hunger to wilder levels.

"Guide me. Take me into your body."

Reaching down, she slid her hand around his erection, glorying in the hot silkiness that sheathed his hunger. His eyes closed, and she drew him closer to herself, twined one leg around his waist as he'd tutored her, and he seated himself with a hiss. Elspeth circled his waist with her other leg, holding him against her.

A small movement, just a nudge by Aeddan, and he entered her body. Smooth friction into her dampness, sensual and hypnotic.

Inside her chest, Elspeth felt the sputter of her heartbeat, blood rushing and thrumming, and her nerves sparked—alive as never before been. The hunger raging as her senses demanded the ultimate pleasure.

"*Aeddan. Aeddan.*" His name became the chant she held onto as they bucked and moved, slid and gripped, each move and undulation more demanding than the last.

Yearning, keening as he kissed her, the wild conflagration between them burning hotter. Scorching them both as they came together.

Elspeth grabbed his shoulder, her fingernails digging deep, seeking purchase as her body splintered around him. "Aeddan!"

He grunted, stilled, shoved deep and hard. She felt him. The final giving as his body released. "*Elspeth.*"

They remained entwined, bodies cooling, until the lethargy filled her, and she slept.

# CHAPTER 19

*I*n the morning when Elspeth rose, Aeddan had already risen and left the chamber. The glow of the night before melted away, and she slumped back against the pillows.

It wasn't a surprise, not really. Things weren't settled between them, and they would leave this morning, back on the open road and heading for Calcutta. If only she could recreate last night when they arrived back at North Point. Yet how would it even be possible? It wasn't like she could ask her man of business to find her a copy of the *Kama Sutra*.

Elspeth rose and set about the task of cleaning and dressing, her mind a whirl, full of memories of what they'd done and said the night before. The abandoned way she'd behaved.

As she left the room, her gaze settled on the book, once more laying on the table where she'd spied it.

Amber was reclined on the lounge in the receiving room, looking paler than the day before.

"Amber, are you unwell?"

The woman smiled wanly. "Oh, I will be. Mornings are a trifle difficult right now. But tell me, did you find everything in the room to your comfort?"

Elspeth's face warmed. "Oh yes."

"Excellent. Did you see the book I had placed in there?"

The nonchalance of Amber's words drew her up short. "You had..."

Amber nodded. "Yes, my dear. I did. What's more, I have a gift for you. Pray, do not open it until you reach your home though." She picked up a package, rectangular and thick. It was wrapped in silken purple cloth.

Elspeth wanted to refuse, sure the gift was too much, but when it was placed in her hands, she knew exactly what it was. "I can't—"

"Please. It is a gift. One my husband and I have other copies of. This is for you."

Elspeth traced the bright design of the cloth, feeling tears burn at her eyelids. If nothing else, she and Aeddan had pleasure. It would be enough.

Amber rubbed her hand over Elspeth's. "The pleasure of your friendship means much to me. You will write?"

Elspeth gazed at the woman on the seat. "I will, Amber. I will."

"Good, that is settled then. Come, eat. Your husband will wish to leave soon, and you will need sustenance for the long ride ahead."

# CHAPTER 20

The sun dipped below the horizon, and Aeddan determined that with the flat area, it would make an adequate campsite. Since the night at the palace, Elspeth had been distracted, and he wondered what had gone on with the princess.

The prince had offered him some useful intelligence though; that there were small groups of English interspersed here and there with Russians traveling the countryside. According to the prince, more than one had made enquiries about an English *memsahib*, a Miss Forster, and described his wife in detail. Since then, he'd requested Elspeth wear a net under her hat to disguise her identity. He just hoped when they reached Calcutta, Lytton had managed to find the ring leaders.

His men took turns at night on guard, not that they'd come across any interesting parties. Only one had contained an Englishman, and he'd been heading off to go tiger hunting. If they were lucky, the man wouldn't meet with any of those who were looking for them.

By day they traveled as swiftly as they could, carrying information pertaining to ruminations of an Indian uprising, the state of India, including the deepening concern of continuing drought that hadn't yet ended. After what he'd seen of the riots in Bombay, it seemed India was becoming a powder keg, ready to erupt at any moment. The sooner Elspeth, Isabelle, and himself were on their way to Shanghai, the better.

They found a small watering hole, diminished and muddy, but it contained enough water for the horses. Another day or two and they'd be home. "What is the water situation, Grundy?"

"Grim, Major," he muttered. "We'll need to ration the water if we don't find a source tomorrow. If we're cautious, we should get home, but there's no water to spare for washing."

Summer was waning, traditionally the wettest time of the year for this area, and in Calcutta the monsoon had already been and gone. The next months were likely to be dangerously dry, increasing the pressure of the government. The constant alertness, concern for his wife, and the information he'd gathered exhausted him...mind, body, and soul.

Turning away, he said over his shoulder, "Fine, inform the men. I'll speak with my wife. Explain the situation. Have the horses watered, and we'll break camp early tomorrow, before dawn. Get as far as we can before the worst of the heat."

Grundy nodded, and Aeddan trudged to the small tent he would share with Elspeth. He entered, surprised to see her brushing out her hair, wisps escaping the long plait she'd pinned to the top of her head each morning.

"Elspeth, there's no water to wash with. We have enough to see us home so long as we ration it cautiously."

She whirled. "You frightened me. What did you say about water?"

He told her of the situation, and she nodded.

"All right then. If things are indeed as bad as you've indicated, would we be better traveling at night and making camp during the day?" she asked. "Surely it would be less taxing for the horses?"

He shook his head. "No. We don't know who we might run into. Under normal circumstances I might agree to that, but I won't take chances with your safety."

Cupping her cheek, his heart raced when she nuzzled in.

"If that's the wisest course of action, Aeddan. How long until we reach Calcutta do you think?"

Grateful that she understood, he dropped down to the pallet on the floor. "If we break camp early tomorrow, before dawn, we should reach the city outskirts within two days. Barring anything happening of course."

Dropping her hairbrush into the small traveling case, she slid down to the pallet beside him, her hands settling in her lap though her expression remained grave. "Do you expect something to happen? You've been very on edge since we left the palace."

"I honestly don't know, Elspeth. If they were going to attack, the time is almost past, yet I'm concerned. You still have the pistol I gave you, don't you?"

"Grundy had one of the men fashion a holster for me." She fumbled in the split skirt and showed him the place she'd secreted it. "I listened when you demanded I keep it on me."

He harrumphed, some of the concern leaching out. He leaned back on the roll that Grundy had rolled into a pillow, and Elspeth followed him down, nestling into his embrace.

"What will happen once we arrive back in Calcutta, Aeddan?"

He sighed. "I will need to report to Lytton, then we'll retrieve Isabelle. When is your ship due back?"

"Ah, now that's difficult to say. The *Zephyr* is our fastest ship, and if it makes a speedy return, I would imagine it will be back in four months, all things being equal. The *Jamestown* is due in three weeks though. It's taking a shipment of spices, textiles, and saltpeter I believe, from the cargo lists I saw before we came away."

"Destination London?"

"I can't remember offhand, but I would presume it would first dock at Falmouth to provision before heading there."

Once more Aeddan harrumphed. "I want you to arrange transport for us, Isabelle, and Grundy aboard the *Jamestown* then. As soon as possible. While I'd rather at this time we were going directly to London, you're still set on Shanghai?"

"Yes. As it is, we're changing our timetable, but it would certainly see us home more swiftly."

They lay still, in companionable silence, and drifted off.

Loud noises, scuffles, and shouts woke him.

Shots echoed and he knifed up, off the pallet, already reaching for his pistol, as Elspeth woke beside him, still dressed in her breeches and white cloth shirt, hair tumbling down. "What's—"

He grabbed her shoulder. "Stay here in the tent. Shoot anyone that isn't Grundy or myself. Promise me, Elspeth?"

She nodded. Even pale and scared, her face was a picture of intense concentration as she reached for the tiny gun he'd given her. His heart shifted in his chest. "Yes. Go."

He rushed out, pistol already primed, summing up the scene in a momentary glance. Fierce fighting swirled around, and it was hard to tell who was friend and foe in the dimness. The glisten of bodies, here and there, interspersed with white shirts, the only clue to who were his men and who wasn't.

The flickering lights were more a problem than assistance, but when the man facing him charged, his sword held high, Aeddan aimed and fired, then waited only long enough to see the man drop before turning.

Loud bangs, thuds, and grunts filled the air. Calls of "to me!" in voices he knew echoed, and Aeddan scrambled, seeking his next opponent.

Sweaty action in the humidity and the scent of coppery blood rising married together with the cacophony of sound brought with it intense clarity. Adrenaline pumped through his veins, surging and pushing him to move faster, hit harder, and aim more surely than ever before.

He grabbed a dropped sword, meeting an attacker, move for move. Seeking an opening.

*Thrust. Parry. Thrust.*

*Slice.* The metal slid between two ribs with a wet, sucking noise, the man crying out as he fell to the ground. The dirt turned slippery as the mixture of mud and blood became a slurry underfoot.

A scream rent the air. Ricocheted in his mind. *"Elspeth!"*

He turned, snarling with rage that someone would attack her. Determined to get to her. Willing to go through anyone as primal reactions kicked in.

*Find her. Protect her.* His heart demanded nothing less. *She's mine!*

He shoved between gyrating bodies, light flickering stronger now as flames licked at bedding, shunted into the cooking fires.

In the glow, he caught sight of two bodies, one twisting and squirming—Elspeth—while the other held her still. *Albermarle!* The mangy cur. One hand curled around her waist, hands splayed as if seeking the mound of her breast, while the other held a stubby and discolored knife at her throat. Her face looked ashen, and her eyes were wide with terror. The quiver of her lips was almost too much for him to bear. The fear on her countenance fed the rage building inside him so that it clawed at his guts, demanding to be set free.

Albermarle crowed and called out, "Look what excellent treasure I've found, Fortescue! Miss Forster is ours for the taking, and since she's been traveling unchaperoned, I'm willing to believe she's—"

"Take your hands off my wife." He barked so loud the man stilled, the smile freezing on his face before sliding away, replaced with an uneasy glare.

"Come now, Fitzsimmons, don't be a dog in the manger." The

man's voice wheedled, "You didn't think we'd give up the chase this easily, did you? We can cut you in though. There's plenty of the money for everyone. The Russians are looking for good people to pass them information. You're in contact with Lytton and the captains from Forster Shipping. The information you've got will garner us all kinds of prizes."

The man had no idea how the disregard for the woman in his grasp enraged him. Aeddan wanted to rip his throat out, but the truth of the matter was, he needed a way to get Elspeth free before he could release the fury ravening within him.

*Find a way to release Elspeth.* The Russians, Fortescue, and Albermarle could go hang. Her safety was his priority, because... The truth dawned, and he strove to block it out, otherwise he'd be seized by terror. She was the key, he finally understood. Shoving that thought away took every ounce of his willpower.

A shadow moved just behind Albermarle. Low and slow movements. Each action rational and considered. *Grundy, by God!* Aeddan wrenched his gaze away from the man moving stealthily forward.

"Leave my wife be. She can be of no use to you."

Albermarle sneered, his whole attention settled on Aeddan, and he could only hope it would be enough to keep the traitor's concentration on him.

"On the contrary, old man. She's of immense use to our cause. The family shipping line? They're running secrets the Colonial Office doesn't trust to The Company. We access those, we know exactly what movements are planned and we sell it to the Russians. The one with the girl is the one with the power. Ergo, the one with the money and influence."

Reality crystalized. Every action seeming to take forever as Elspeth growled and stomped down hard with her boot-shod foot just as Albermarle ceased speaking. Her howl was lost as Albermarle screeched with pain. Next, she bared her teeth and bit deep on his hand, drawing blood as he attempted to yank away.

Albermarle swung as if to cuff her, but she caught sight and moved, the blow glancing off her, although Aeddan heard her hiss as he advanced, arm drawn back with the sword, ready to hack at the man anywhere and any way he could. *I'll make the bastard pay!*

The shadow erupted from the dark. *Grundy.* Intent on saving Elspeth, who'd already freed herself.

He and Grundy moved in concert. The man didn't stand a chance as Aeddan slashed at him, Albermarle jumping backward into Grundy's embrace. The wiry batman had Albermarle on the ground in a flash as Aeddan clawed at his belt, wrenching it off so he could tie the man up.

"Get me rope!" Aeddan's bellow echoed in the sudden quiet, and he realized in that instant the battle was done.

Cord was thrust into his grasp, and Fortescue, sniveling with pain after being sliced by one of Aeddan's men, was dragged to a stake in the middle of the camp area, as was Albermarle, both men bound and gagged. Then his men rounded up the injured, dead, and dying.

Elspeth didn't cry. In stark relief, he noted the starch in his wife, the straight back and tight lips.

She didn't break. The men came and went around her, and they noted that too. Pride welled up, until he slid his arm around her shoulder.

Elspeth remained stiff. Controlled.

"Come to the tent, Elspeth."

Wordlessly, she followed him, and the flap closed with a snap.

She whirled, threw herself into his embrace, and the dam broke. Tears soaking his shirt, the sound broken.

"Elspeth. Shhh..." He soothed and rubbed her back, letting the storm pass, understanding that she needed the release.

When the worst subsided, she slumped against him, and he bent, picked her up, and carried her to the pallet. There were tasks to be completed, but his wife needed him now. Her needs couldn't be ignored.

"Elspeth?"

"You... You have things to do, and I'll... I can wait for you." The sound of her broken voice scored him like shards of glass. Once more he vowed that the two men outside would pay.

"If you need me, I'll stay."

Elspeth tugged away, some of the starch returning to her spine. "No. Your men need you now. I'll wait here for you." She sat up and wiped the traces of tears from her cheeks. "You've got the ring leaders, and I won't let you or your men down by appearing weak in front of them."

Though Aeddan hadn't thought it possible, she rose in his estimation. "You're sure?"

"Absolutely. Go do your duty then return."

He turned then whirled back, giving her a quick, hard kiss to reassure them both before tugging away. He didn't want to leave her there by herself but was also aware that his men needed his direction.

# CHAPTER 21

*C*alcutta rose in the distance, the white of the built environment a welcome sight after the privations of their journey. Weeks on the road and the horrific attack left Elspeth struggling to maintain her composure. But she held onto her sanity with a rigid grasp.

She drooped in her saddle, aching from the rough handling she'd received at Albermarle's hands, while her equilibrium was dented as well. Aeddan had remained close by, always solicitous, as she fought to maintain the wall of brittle composure. Elspeth longed for the privacy afforded by a bedroom. Somewhere to hide away and lick her wounds.

Grundy kept his distance—supervising the handling of Fortescue and Albermarle—and she glanced in the direction of Aeddan. He'd ridden ahead. She might be surrounded by their guard, but she'd never felt so alone.

"North Point isn't far away, Elspeth."

The haze of pre-dawn light they'd left in changed to day, but it wasn't the heavy, sultry atmosphere of May and June, so she welcomed the hours of light.

The terrain stretched out before them, leading to the

metropolis, and beyond that, the residential areas. In the distance, ship masts appeared like white puffs on the ocean. Her memories of the scent of sea water was a balm to her soul.

They plodded on, time passing in a fugue. Dirt tracks gave way to formed roads, and they entered the government district sometime around midday. Wide roads led them to the imposing structure of Government House. Aeddan had sent a man ahead to apprise the guards, and they were met just inside the ornate metal gates, and their two prisoners handed to the authorities. Elspeth kept herself aloof, wanting nothing more to do with the men.

Their guards drifted away, the horses whinnying as the men alighted, and Elspeth waited in silence until Aeddan joined her. "Grundy will follow us later. Come, let's go home."

"The men?"

"Their task is complete, Elspeth. Come, you need rest."

She followed his lead, letting Sana pick her way through the streets. The kaleidoscope of colors and humanity ebbed and flowed, and she let it ripple around her. Her focus remained on maintaining serenity until she was alone. In her mind, a vision of the bathing room off her chamber rose. If only she could restrain her emotions until then.

The façade of North Point appeared, a two-storey house, colonial in style and wooden in construction with wide verandas and shrubby garden beds came into view.

Staff hurried to meet them, grabbing for the reins, and Elspeth gladly handed Sana's over. She urgently craved the tranquility that lay within the house.

She dropped to the ground before Aeddan could assist, and with a quick "thank you" to the staff, she made her way to the door with swift steps on the gravel drive. Tears burned her eyelids.

"Elspeth?" Aeddan called, but she scurried on, fearing that to turn now, to surrender to his attention, would be her undoing.

The door opened without a sound, and she shoved inside, the echoes of Aeddan's footsteps dogging her.

"Wait!" he called, and she swallowed the sob that rose, stilling at the base of the curving stairway.

"Please. I can't. Not now." She turned to let him glimpse the ravages inside her, and he groaned.

Aeddan swooped in and gathered her close, then moved, taking the stairs two at a time.

She burrowed in, unable to hold out any longer against the clamor of her emotions. Fright and rage warred with desperation and loss of control.

"I thought we were going to die, Aeddan. That our life would be over and I'd never have the..." Shaking her head, she broke off the words, shattered that she'd lost control, however briefly.

At the chamber, he opened the door and carried her in. If the staff had spied her, or heard any of her words, she didn't know. All that mattered was the steady thumping of his heartbeat against her ear.

"Elspeth, look at me."

Aeddan spoke urgently, and unable to deny him, she complied.

"We need to talk. Words I should have said weeks ago. Things I kept..." With a savage shake of his head, he sighed. "I was a fool to think I should keep anything from you. I wanted you, Elspeth. From the first moment on the *Zephyr*, I desired you. Burned for you."

Head in a whirl, she stared at him, his face a study of harsh planes, lips compressed.

"When they had you, when Albermarle hit you, I wanted to tear him limb from limb. Inside me, the primal creature, the one who worshipped your body, took over. I wanted to kill him. Because he hurt you. Frightened you. Terrorized you."

This creature holding her, the man stripped bare, amazed her.

"I hated the fact I hadn't been honest. That I didn't tell you my feelings. I was frightened before, but it was nothing to the terror that held me in its fist. I told myself I could lie. I could keep the truth out of our union."

Her heart plunged to her stomach. *Does he plan to send me away?*

Aeddan reached out and softly caressed the side of her cheek. His thumb settled on her lips, and God help her, even now they opened, seeking the taste and feel of this man.

"I should have told you I loved you, Elspeth."

Shock rippled.

*Love?*

"Do you..." He glanced away, the tide of red cresting his cheeks like flags of high emotion. "I can't make you love me. But if you ever could, I'd be—"

*He loves me!*

"I will always love you, Aeddan. You're the part of me that was missing. The fire in my soul."

$\sim$

*T*riumph suffused Aeddan. This strong and amazing woman returned his love, and the knowledge humbled him. Yet, even in the middle of his victory, there was still a seed of disquiet.

"That's not all that upset you, was it?" he asked.

Elspeth squirmed in his grasp, turned away from him. The action cutting him deeply.

"You said that Lytton made you marry me, Aeddan. It gutted me, and with the attack and not knowing... I was trying to keep myself safe. Protect myself from hurt and drowning in my fears." The way her voice choked had him cursing the memory of those words. On the rock that day. When she'd walked away.

"*Elspeth*..." What could he say that would explain she'd truly only heard part of the truth? "Yes, Lytton did order me to protect you, and after the library, there was an understanding that I'd marry you. But that wasn't everything. It doesn't explain that I wanted you already. Had settled on marrying you once we'd arrived in Calcutta, and was seeking a way to bring that about."

With a shaking hand, he cupped her chin, making her face him. He gazed deep into her eyes, hoping she'd read the truth.

"I should have told you everything up front. I didn't want to lose you, and things moved so quick. So, I grabbed the chance, Elspeth. I made mistakes, but now we can fix them, with everything out in the open. If you'll let me."

The moment stretched, skating over his nerves until he was sure she'd refute his claims.

A tiny tear, diamond-bright, flittered on her lash. "I wanted to trust you, Aeddan." The thickness of her voice came close to unmanning him. "It's hard. I'm seven and twenty. Past the time when girlish dreams should be coming true. I'm mature and not in the least adventuresome—"

"All evidence to the contrary, my love."

Her laugh was more a sputter at his outburst.

"Perhaps. But I thought I'd put such dreams away. I'd come in search of information, and yes, passion too. I'd thought perhaps a dalliance was the most I could hope for and there you were. On the *Zephyr*. You caught me when Isabelle was still sick and I was off-balance. Then to hear you, that day? My world crashed down, and I was sure the best I could hope for was emptiness in our marriage—without hope for love. It hurt."

His heart cracked at the knowledge he'd caused her such pain. *I'll make it up to her.*

"Forgive me, Elspeth. I never meant to do that."

This time, Elspeth closed the distance between them, laying her lips against his, her palm cradling his face, the pads of her fingertips soft and tender. The gentle caress of her lips against his burned him, then she tugged away.

"Amber gave me a gift before we left."

He blinked at the change of subject. "A gift?"

"Yes. In my saddlebag. Would you find it for me?"

The lightning change of mood surprised Aeddan, yet he'd vowed to show her his trustworthiness. "I'll have a bath drawn for you then." He slid her to the bed, rose. "I'll retrieve the item."

"It's wrapped, Aeddan. In silk."

He retreated from the room, stopping only to call for the bathwater, and hurried down the stairs in the direction of the stables.

The saddlebags were placed on top of the saddles, perched on hay bales. He gathered them up as Grundy came barreling around the corner. "Sir?"

"My wife's saddlebags. She has something in one she requires."

"Let me."

Grundy moved forward, but Aeddan stopped him. "No. I have what she's after." He held up the silk-wrapped parcel, the size and shape of a book. His breathing seized. *Surely not!*

His thoughts skittered, and while he couldn't be sure definitively to what he held, excitement grew in his mind. *If this is what I believe it to be...* The thoughts matched increased eager growth that suddenly made itself known in his breeches.

"Grundy, have a meal prepared then send the staff home for the day." They'd cope without others for a night, and if this parcel was what he hoped, he didn't want any interruption as they explored what lay between the covers.

Grundy stared at him as if he'd run mad. "Sir? Miss Isabelle is due on the morrow as you instructed and—"

"Good night, Grundy."

∼

*T*he staff disappeared once they'd drawn a deep and fragrant bath. The scent of candles, sandalwood and patchouli the maid had lit emitted the most decadent of aromas. In the daylight hours as they flickered and danced—erotic and sensual. *Truly this is wanton in the daytime.* Though many of the sensual delights Aeddan had introduced her to probably fell into that category too. She thrust the thought aside.

The door slid shut with a whisper, and she dropped the robe from her shoulders. The mirror on the wall reflected the color of her skin along with the dips and hollows of her body. Elspeth stopped, her hands running down her nude form, no longer embarrassed by the act. Aeddan had taught her that passion and sensuality were not just acceptable, but a gift. Something to be savored and enjoyed.

The last time she'd been here, she'd scurried through the ritual of bathing, eyes averted from the view in the mirror. The looking glass then had seemed inappropriate, yet now...

"Perhaps my view of life has changed." Her mind cast back to her parents' bathing room. There'd been no such item in there, leading her to wonder if indeed this was an unusual item in a married woman's apartment. A small titter escaped. *No wonder so few marriages seem fulfilled, if they did not enjoy such abandoned intimacies.* She sobered for a moment. *Just as mine could have been if we hadn't spoken freely.*

Turning away, Elspeth moved to the tub and stepped in, her body relaxing in the warm water as it slid over her skin. As if she were ready to float away.

The tub was deep and long, and she stretched, resting her arms on the side of the metal, her head lying on the lip where a towel had been laid. Eyes closed, she inhaled the essence, noting the heady scents of neroli, rose, and jasmine from the oils the maid had poured in.

Her gaze flashed to the doorway at the crashing sound of

wood against plaster. Aeddan strode inside, his eyes turning smoky as he settled his gaze on her. "I found the gift, Elspeth."

She smiled, knowing full well it was filled with mischief. "Did you? And you opened it?"

He cocked his head to one side. "No. I thought we might do that later. *Together.*"

Promise lay in his words, and her stomach lurched, her mind returning to the last time they'd perused it together. The emotions and the physical acts they'd enjoyed.

"Indeed?"

Without a word, Aeddan reached for the buttons of his shirt, and Elspeth was spellbound, watching him flick at the tiny closures until his chest was bared to her sight. Delicious skin bronzed where the sun had caught it, and pale in other areas.

Next, he divested himself of his boots, careful actions as he stared at her, aware that her body had started to prepare for what lay ahead.

Her mouth dried when his hands turned to his belt, understanding his intentions. She gulped for air as he hooked his thumbs under his breeches and undergarments. Then he stood before her. Naked. All man and all hers.

She gazed her fill, her eyes roaming up and down the planes of his body. Taking in the dark hair at the juncture of this legs and the immense erection.

Hunger roared, but she had to hold onto her sanity. "The door. You should lock it."

He smiled, his eyes ablaze. "I've given the staff the rest of the day off. There's no one else here, Elspeth."

He advanced, loped toward the tub and climbed in, settling at the other end, so his legs bracketed hers.

*Decadent.* No other word described the act of bathing together in the daylight.

The water rippled, the warm swell lapping at her body,

nipples budding tightly in response while her sex ached, ready for fulfillment.

"Will..." Talking and thought were difficult as her brain turned sluggish with desire. "Will it always be like this?"

"I hope so, Elspeth."

His foot moved, glancing up the side of her leg, and she moaned, as her body reacted intuitively. She slid a little deeper into the water, adjusting her posture and wondering if it were indeed possible in the tub.

"Aeddan?"

The breath in her lungs fled as he reached for her hand. "Would you be interested in another lesson?"

*Yes! Oh yes!* "Please?" she answered with a croak, and he reached for her, taking her hand and pulling her upright.

"Not here though. Not this time."

*So, it is possible.*

Elspeth made to crawl into his lap but he placed a soft finger against her lips. "Come, let me bathe you. Turn around."

Without answering, she maneuvered so her back rested against his chest.

Dribbling water down her shoulders, he ministered, "Loving is an art, Elspeth. Lovers should be aware and responsive to the needs of the other." His hands settled at her waist, and he pulled her so she could feel the length of him against her buttocks. His chin rested on her shoulder, the whisper of his words teasing the sensitive skin there. "It is giving. Eager to share its bounty."

Elspeth shivered as his hands closed over her breasts, his thumbs gently teasing the tight nubs. His legs held her immobile, as she arched back, fine tremors of hunger zinging through her body.

"Aeddan?"

"Just feel, my love. Breathe deeply and concentrate on how you feel when I touch you." One hand moved down to her ribcage. "Feel it here. The pleasure and warmth."

Her eyes fluttered closed. "I... I do, Aeddan."

"And here." His hand settled on the curve of her belly, which quivered with excitement. Heat settling in her stomach as she gave herself up to the pleasure.

When his hand slid down to her mound, she arched up, the water shifting like a wave which licked at her nipples on its return, and she moaned. Desire was a ravenous creature within her.

"Aeddan?" Her cry echoed in the silence.

The deep chuckle and reverberations echoed inside her mind. "There's more, my love. And no need to rush."

He released her, reached for the soap as she cracked her eyes open.

A demand rose to her lips, heavy with frustration, but it melted away when he captured her gaze—hooded and hungry. He rubbed the cake between his hands. "This is part of the ritual too. Let me bathe you, my love. Prepare you for the night ahead."

When he touched her she jolted, the slide of fingers and palms over damp skin reigniting the fire that had dimmed when he'd moved away.

"Your body is a temple. Perfectly built for my loving." His words drugged her, pulling her deeper into the sensual haze. "When you're ready, you'll show me just the same. Gift me with the words."

She opened her mouth then closed it again.

"One day, soon. But today, let me teach you more. School you in arts you've not yet imagined."

~

*A*fter they moved from the bath to the bedroom, he led her by the hand to the edge of the bed, allowing time for her hunger to abate slightly. "Come, let us inspect this gift from your friend."

He gestured to the parcel on the bed, and all the while, her body throbbed with hunger for Aeddan.

"We could—"

The kiss he stilled her words with scorched. His tongue thrust deeply inside the cavern of her mouth, and she pushed closer, skin against skin.

He tugged away, framing her face with unsteady hands. "Soon. Come, my love, let us see this gift."

Her moue of regret was met with a bark of laughter.

She sighed and followed him onto the mattress, settling against the mounded pillows as he unfolded the length of fine, purple cloth.

"She wrapped it in a sari," he murmured. Once he had finished unwrapping it, the book of pleasure they'd seen at the palace was revealed.

"Amber told me they had other copies. It was a gift of friendship. She's lonely and I think *enceinte*." Pregnancy wasn't discussed between husbands and wives openly, but with Aeddan, and the things they did, if felt natural. Snuggling closer to Aeddan, her body cooling, it felt important to tell him what she'd discovered.

"Indeed. She and the prince are very much in love. Their child will be cherished. Just as much as any from our union will be."

His words, spoken quietly, surprised her. "Aeddan, if I were expecting, we wouldn't be able to..."

"Shh. We can cross that bridge when we arrive there."

A vision rose, and while she wanted it, could almost touch the tiny breathing bundle, they weren't ready. Not yet, so she blinked, banishing it...for now.

Aeddan opened the cover. Paging through to where they'd ceased last time. "This one intrigues me, Elspeth." The image was of a couple, entwined intimately, his hands at her waist, the man seated within the woman.

"*Oh...*"

Again, her body quickened. Aeddan pulled her into his embrace, laying the book aside, then reaching for her leg. Holding it up so he could nestle there, his erection nudging her core.

"Let me try something?" The timbre of his voice was rough and hungry.

Elspeth couldn't deny him, her body ablaze already. "Yes, Aeddan."

"Every time I look at the illustrations, I don't see them, Elspeth. I see us. You and me, entwined."

She melted inside and knew he felt it too. His words filling the emptiness within her so that all there was room for was him. The other half of her soul.

"Your honey tastes so sweet and it's already coating me, my love. Let me enter your temple. Let me fill you."

Her body bowed, so he slid within.

She vibrated in his arms as they moved slowly. "Every time is better. More mystical." His mutter was lost as she moaned, starving for the pleasure that was ready to explode within her.

"Aeddan? Let me feel you." She dragged her fingers up his chest to grip at his shoulders, demanding more. "Let me feel your hardness. Your strength. Fill me."

Every caress heightened her awareness. Her body so hot she would surely combust. They undulated—rocking and yearning against each other until the wave crashed over her. Her cry echoed, matched only by his.

The racing of their hearts slowing as they held together.

# CHAPTER 22

*T*he journey to the *Jamestown* took time to arrange. Elspeth used the break to finalize the initial purpose of her visit to India. Time passed quickly, meeting with her man of business and inspecting the bales of cloth that arrived. Ledgers required inspection, and invoices awaiting authorization were dealt with. She placed more orders, able to specify the types and lengths of material, and gave instructions for a new supplier to be added—the one who'd created the fine purple silk wound around a book hidden carefully in her trunk.

Isabelle returned from her visit with Lady Manton, full of fire and excitement. In her free time, she chattered about the balls and outings they'd undertaken, and the people they'd met and interacted with, including the vicereine, Lady Lytton. "Lady Lytton is indeed a wonder, Elspeth. She's involved in all manner of ideas. Of course, her little girl is just the sweetest, little thing!"

However, Isabelle still kept a watchful eye on Aeddan and became more subdued. Something that Elspeth mulled over with concern.

On the arrival of the *Jamestown*, though, Isabelle waited just as impatiently as Elspeth. Inspection of the vessel and reorganization were handled by Isabelle in her usual unruffled fashion. This allowed Elspeth and Aeddan to conclude their business free of concern for their voyage, though Aeddan did mention it was a trifle unusual to have a female in charge of such matters.

He remained busy, settling his affairs, returning the lease on North Point and disbanding all the servants, except for Jacinthe and Grundy. Jacinthe had been overcome by the offer made for her to become Elspeth's official lady's maid since Anara wouldn't travel with them. It was a title Jacinthe would never have aspired to.

One evening, just before they returned to Spence's Hotel, Elspeth enquired, "Isabelle, was there no girl among the staff who would be suitable for your personal lady's maid?" Finding space aboard for a second maid would have posed problems, but they weren't insurmountable.

"No, Elspeth. I feel sure though that until we reach Shanghai Jacinthe will cater for both of us admirably."

Elspeth simply shrugged, allowing her sister that latitude. Aboard the ship, there'd be little enough work for the young girl.

On the ship, Jacinthe and Isabelle took up residence in one cabin while the captain's quarters were made ready for Elspeth and Aeddan.

Early on the evening before sailing, Elspeth jumped at the rap on the door. "Come in!"

Isabelle entered the room and placed a wooden box on the small ledge beside the bed. "What's that, Elspeth?"

"It's a gift. From my husband." Elspeth ran her finger lightly over the wood, aware that inside lay oils, scented and meant for her continuing 'education' as her husband archly described it.

"You're happy, aren't you? India was everything you asked for and more."

Elspeth sighed, unable to ignore the longing in her sister's voice. It hurt to realize that she'd found a treasure here, yet her sister remained unattached.

"I truly am, Isabelle. Tell me, for all the events you attended, was there no man who intrigued you?"

Isabelle slumped down on the bunk and shook her head. "None that drew me the way Aeddan did you. Am I going to be the only one left a spinster, Elspeth? Where is my happy situation?" Despair colored her words.

Elspeth moved to embrace her sister, but Isabelle shook her head.

"That was unfair of me. Forgive me. I just... Maybe in Shanghai I'll meet a man. One who completes me." Isabelle rose, wiping away her tears. "The future is for looking forward to, and I'm sure this voyage won't be as exciting or traumatic as the last. So, tell me, when is Aeddan due aboard?"

Elspeth inspected her sister's face. She'd chosen to focus on what was positive, but Elspeth resolved that if Isabelle didn't meet someone in Shanghai, she'd do her best on their return to England to find a suitable gentleman for her sister. Isabelle deserved a happy future.

"He's meeting with Lytton now, making his final report and finalizing his commission."

They'd told Isabelle most of the truth, agreeing to only share the facts about the courier duties of Forster Shipping captains when at sea.

"I can't believe we've been here five months. It's gone so quickly." Her sister glanced out the window, her gaze pensive.

Isabelle was right. The five months since she'd arrived in India, the events that culminated in her very happy marriage had whipped it on with fervor.

A commotion at the gangway caught her attention and she glanced outward, seeking the source. There was Grundy and Aeddan, coming aboard. She moved from the cabin to meet her husband.

With the cargo loaded, it was time to leave. To another adventure and the next port.

# BIOCYBE BY IMOGENE NIX

Levia scanned the long line of other hopefuls entering the testing chamber. The large building in the center of town was cold, and she dragged her wrap around her body, even as she craned her head, looking to the high ceiling. She'd never before had an occasion to enter the testing complex, yet she'd seen the lines of teenagers every time they passed the building.

Once she'd asked her parents why the teens were lined up and her mother's face had shuttered. Her stepfather had just shaken his head and growled. They'd stopped her questions with a carefully uttered, "You'll know soon enough, Levia." The pain in her mother's eyes had been enough to shush her questions. For endless months afterward, her parents had traveled different routes to the educational facility she attended and Levia lost interest in the puzzle of that building.

Now, as she looked around, remembering that long ago spring day, it was her opportunity to find out. But she felt a surge of concern at what lay ahead. She likely wasn't the only one, given that there were probably two to three hundred seventeen-year-olds gathered in the one place. Ahead of her, she caught sight of a couple of girls, their arms linked together and wide smiles on their faces. Scanning the crowd, she became aware that, by far, a majority of those gathered displayed both fear and trepidation.

"All female subjects will enter through doors three, six, and seven. All male subjects will enter through gates four, eight, and ten." The speaker above her was loud, and she jumped before checking the numbers etched on the black metal sign over her head.

The massive doors beside her swung open, and now an uncertain silence reigned. Many of the youngsters hung back, clearly discomforted by whatever testing regime lay ahead. This was where they'd been told their futures would be determined.

"Oh gosh, I hope they only have an aptitude and psych eval. I don't think..." Levia turned to see the white face of the girl behind her. The girl had uttered what many must silently be thinking.

Levia dragged an unsteady breath in, her hand resting flat against the plane of her belly as she looked around. No one had entered yet. It was clear many were on the verge of taking the step, but still they hung back.

She straightened her shoulders. "I'm not afraid." It was always wiser to approach things head-on, she believed. When her biological father had died, she'd been one of the few to view his capsule before it was sent into the massive gray structure built to accommodate those who'd moved onto the next life realm.

Her legs shook as she wobbled toward the entrance. Beyond the doorway, she spied sealed cubicles and her heart stuttered. Why cubicles? Usually testing—med and psych—were in eval-units, hidden only by billowing white curtains. She glanced back, noting that others had taken the first step.

"Move along, subjects." Once again, the androgynous voice of the address system blared.

Of course, given it was her seventeenth anniversary of birth, she was technically considered an adult now.

She thought longingly of baby Rald and her half-sister, Elda, waiting at home for her to return, and the celebrations to be held that night. That made her smile. She would need to make them proud of her.

She entered a row and the tall Educational Specialist, the edu-specs as her peers laughingly called them, stopped her. "Present your credentials to the scanner."

She'd done this many times since the tiny implant had been slipped below the dermal layer of her skin at birth. The small unit in her wrist heated as her details were checked.

"Enter the first cubicle, Levia Endrado, and follow the instructions to complete your assessment."

Thus dismissed, Levia moved to the first unit, laid her palm against the scanner, and the door slid open soundlessly.

"Welcome, Levia Endrado. Take your place in the eval-unit." The soft contralto of the voice echoed after the door closed silently behind her.

"What are you evaluating?" Her voice was breathy, and she peered around.

"Your skills—physical and psychological. Your emotional and medical status. Your educational attainment levels."

It was an answer that shed little insight into the many things she was hungry to know. "Why do all seventeen year olds—"

"Take a seat, Levia. Then we may begin your testing." If she'd expected an answer, she was sadly mistaken, she considered sourly. She dropped into the seat, the soft leather-like surface molding to her body. "Levia Endrado, you are required to remove all non-specified apparel." She jolted in the chair. "It's cold." "The temperature will be amended. Remove the non-specified apparel." Her misgivings grew as she dragged off the light wrap she'd brought with her, and then threw it to the floor at the side of the unit. "We will begin, Levia Endrado. At any time, should you experience any malfunctions of the unit, simply depress the red button." It glowed and she grimaced. Levia reclined against the chair and waited for the testing to begin. The first examination was based on her understanding of the political system, where she saw herself, and her knowledge of the rights and responsibilities accorded through citizenship of both her planet and the commonwealth.

The second test was mathematical and scientific proficiency. It felt like hours had passed by the time she'd finished, and she lay limp on the seat, exhausted.

"Levia Endrado, you may rise. The sanitary unit will emerge once you trigger the yellow button at the door. Should you require refreshment, press the blue button and a restorative will be made available."

"Can I leave?" "Negative, Levia Endrado. Your needs will be catered for in this capsule." "Why?" Her voice hitched and true fear rose for the first time. Why did they keep her in the alcove? "All will be revealed at the end of the testing cycle." Levia looked at the now empty screen before hurling a curse word. It was met with silence. The urgent throb of her bladder reminded her that she needed to use the facilities, so, with

a sigh, she rose and clambered from the seat. After attending to the needs of her body, she walked around the unit, peering at the door, but it was obviously programmed remotely. She poked and prodded, but it made no difference. With a huff, she headed back to the chair.

The moment she'd settled in, the viewing screen shone bright. "Welcome back, Levia. The next sequence will evaluate your psychological reflexes, then that will be followed up with the general knowledge portion of the evaluation."

"When can I leave?" It seemed better to ask bluntly, she told herself.

"Once the examination is completed. After the next set of evaluations, you will be subjected to the physical aspect."

"Then I can go home?"

"Levia Endrado, you will now complete the psychological test. This will be undertaken by one of the center's personal evaluators."

She frowned. Personal evaluators? She bit her lip, and the sting reminded her that this wasn't something to joke about. In her seventeen years, she'd only heard of personal evaluators being brought in once before, and that was when one of the girls at her academy had been in a serious accident. Both legs were amputated and her body's ability to keep her alive had been gravely compromised. Her peers had been informed that the girl had requested the assessment before she could request her support systems be disconnected.

"Levia Endrado, are you ready to recommence processing?" The emotionless voice echoed once more and she gulped.

"Yes."

Available from Beachwalk Press
http://www.beachwalkpress.com

Direct Autographed Books
http://bit.ly/BioCybe

# INHERITANCE OF THE BLOOD BY IMOGENE NIX

*The burning at the back of her neck warned she was being watched. A quick glance didn't clarify it. Instead, she turned around in time to see her mother's face, pale. "Mama?" She took a step forward, but her grandfather snatched her wrist.*

*The grip was painful, and Kira stilled. "Let your parents talk."*

*She didn't know what the topic of conversation was, but it couldn't be good.*

*The dappled sunlight seemed cooler than before.*

Her father crooked his forefinger at her grandfather while they stood there. For a moment she wished Vasya had come with them, but he had to work. Just the thought of her new husband warmed Kira.

She only had a few minutes to contemplate her newly defined status as a married woman, when her grandfather pulled at her hand. "Come with me." He tugged and, confused, Kira allowed herself to be towed away.

A glance at her parents' faces stole any feeling of well-being. "Grandfather?"

"Shh, my love. You must go." His grip was implacable and his face stern, but he shivered.

"What are you doing? Where are you taking me, Grandfather?"

They moved rapidly through the village they'd visited to sell their wares just that morning, and for the first time since they'd arrived in the market place she felt fear. What was wrong? Was it something to do with Vasya?

"You are in danger. We must send you away." The words confused her further. Send her away? Danger?

"Where is Vasya?" She stumbled over a stone, but he kept tugging her onwards.

With a quick glance around, he hauled her into a dirty laneway between the buildings. Kira gasped, trying to drag air into her starving lungs. "There's no time. We must get you away."

A nondescript shopfront lay ahead, and he pushed on the door. It rattled and opened with a loud groan. "Andre? Andre, are you here?"

An older man shuffled into the room, bent nearly double from the weight of the load on his back. "Marat? What do you want?"

"My granddaughter. They are coming for her and us. Get her away. Take her now, while you can."

The man's face clouded over. "Are you sure?"

"Grandfather, where is Vasya?" Fright had the blood in her veins pounding.

"Hush, my precious. Andre will see you well." He turned. "What-

ever it takes, Andre. Take her now." With surprising speed, her grandfa-*
*ther whirled and was gone.*

The man, Andre, eyed her. "Come this way, child. There is no time*
*to be lost."*

*Eleven years later*

The tattoo of her heart and cry of terror woke her, as they usually did. Once again, as she had since that rapid flight from those who sought her, she found herself in a lonely bed. Hundreds of miles away from everything she'd dreamed of, in a house she'd built for them to share. As always, it left her wishing that Vasya had fled with her.

Instead, here she was, exiled without her husband. With a sob, she rolled over and let the tears fall.

Available from Beachwalk Press
**books2read.com/IOTB**

Direct Autographed Copy

http://bit.ly/2w6g4K6

# ALSO BY IMOGENE NIX

## Warriors of the Elector

- Star of Ishtar
- Starline
- Starfire
- Star of the Fleet
- Starburst
- The Star of Eternity

The Star of Ishtar & Starline - Print

Starfire & Star of the Fleet - Print

Starburst & The Star of Eternity - Print

## Blood Secrets

- The Blood Bride
- The Illuminated Witch
- The Sorcerer's Touch

## Reunion Trilogy

- War's End
- The Assassin
- Executing Justice

The Reunion Trilogy in Paperback

## Sex Love & Aliens

- Tangled Webs
- False Webs
- Covert Webs

## 21st Testing Protocol

- Cyborg: Redux (Not Yet Released)
- Children Of A Greater Evil (Not Yet Released)

## Celtic Cupid Trilogy

- Blame The Wine
- A Stranger's Embrace
- Revenge On Cupid

## Single Titles

The Chocolate Affair

A Sapphire for Karina

BioCybe

Hesparia's Tears

Tomorrow's Promise

A Bar In Paris

Inheritance Of The Blood

The Plan

Loving Memories

The Reset (2018)

Hero of Heartbreak Hill (2018 - Kiss Me: An Asian hero boxed set)

## Non Fiction

Self Publishing: Absolute Beginners Guide (With Suzi Love)

**Also books by Ciara Cave**

25 Curated Ways To Get Rid Of Telemarketers

Book Signings for Absolute Beginners

# ABOUT THE AUTHOR

Imogene is published in a range of romance genres including Paranormal, Science Fiction and Contemporary. She is mainly published in the UK and USA due to the nature of her tales.

In 2010, Imogene Nix (the pen name not Imogene herself) was born. Imogene sat down and worked tirelessly for 3 months culminating in the book Starline, which became the first in a trilogy titled, "Warriors of the Elector." Since then she's had over 30 titles published and is now focusing on hybridising herself - with a mixture of traditionally published and self-published works.

In fact, she's taking control of many of her back catalogue books, which are slowly re-releasing as self-published titles.

Imogene is a member of a range of professional organisations world wide, and believes in the mantra of mentoring and paying it forward and is actively involved in mentorship (through NaNo-Wrimo and her vlog: In The Chair With Imogene Nix) and tutoring of new and upcoming authors.

In her spare time she loves to drink coffee, wine & eat chocolate and is parenting 2 spoiled dogs and a ferocious cat along with her husband and 2 human daughters and looks forward to weekends away with her husband in their caravan "The Seven Year Hitch!" Do look forward to her caravan romance at some point!

*To Contact Imogene*

www.imogenenix.net
imogene@imogenenix.net

facebook.com/ImogeneNix
twitter.com/ImogeneNix
instagram.com/ImogeneNix

www.ingramcontent.com/pod-product-compliance
Lightning Source LLC
Chambersburg PA
CBHW071605110726
47908CB00007B/2258

www.ingramcontent.com/pod-product-compliance
Lightning Source LLC
Chambersburg PA
CBHW071556110726
47908CB00007B/2122